The Peace Mission Arrives on Planet Eldry

"There! There's the base, Friend; see it?"

"No. Oh, you mean that light spot? Where are the landing pads?"

"There are no pads; the volcanic plate under the ice will hold the ship anywhere. But see those little lines not far from the shelter? They're blast shields, to allow us to land near the building. Just line up on one and set us down."

The landing was steady; but when the engines had stopped, and all systems were idling, a rumbling vibration continued.

"Did I leave something on?" Friend asked.

Firemaker's face betrayed concern. "The ground is shaking," he said. "I don't know whether our landing set it off, or—"

"It's a quake?" Friend whispered, wide-eyed.

We will send you a free catalog on request. Any titles not in your local book store can be purchased by mail. Send the price of the book plus 50¢ shipping charge to Leisure Books, Two Park Avenue, New York, New York 10016, Attention: Premium Sales Department.

Titles currently in print are available for industrial and sales promotion at reduced rates. Address inquiries to Nordon Publications, Inc., Two Park Avenue, New York, New York 10016, Attention: Premium Sales Department.

GODS IN A VORTEX

David Houston

Illustrated by the author

LEISURE BOOKS • NEW YORK CITY

Also by David Houston:
ALIEN PERSPECTIVE

A LEISURE BOOK

Published by

Nordon Publications, Inc.
Two Park Avenue
New York, N.Y. 10016

Copyright © 1979, by Nordon Publications, Inc.

Music and Illustrations Copyright © 1979
by David Houston

All rights reserved
Printed in the United States

**for
John, Kerry and Tom.**
Many, many years ago, we invented a little universe which may yet turn out to be *the* universe.

CONTENTS

1. At Ayat's Tree 13
2. Isle Firemaker 17
3. Incident at Retribution Square 25
4. The Fate of *Watchful Monz* 29
5. At the Inn of Three Foxes 31
6. How the Gods Came to
   the Cathedral Ayat 35
7. Sky Tinsmith, Infidel 40
8. Where the Sewers Lead 47
9. The Invisible Arm of Parliament 49
10. Weaver's Inn of the Frog 53
11. A Year in the Vortex 59
12. The Warehouse 66
13. The Flying Pig 71
14. A Gull Envious of the Bears 74
15. The Hero and the Anarchist 76
16. The Reluctant Hatchling 79
17. The Glen 83
18. The Congress of Ky—First Session 86
19. Sleep in a Sanctuary 91
20. The Congress of Ky—Second Session 94
21. Night of the Black Balloons 104
22. The Congress of Ky—Third Session 108

23.	Escape	113
24.	The Benefactor	120
25.	On a Mission of Conciliation	126
26.	On a Mission of Power	130
27.	On a Mission of Conquest	131
28.	Ky—Legacy of Malefactors	133
29.	The Children of the Plague	135
30.	Masters Among the Masterless	145
31.	Two Women, Half a Man	150
32.	An Eccentric in the Metropolis of the Insane	152
33.	Nyasport Mandates a Mission	158
34.	Annihilation With a Three-Year Guarantee	167
35.	Weightless Cargo	170
36.	In the Vortex	177
37.	Eldry	188
38.	Captured by Captives	195
39.	The End of Eldry Base	200
40.	A Walk in the Garden	209
41.	Forest Singer	215

ILLUSTRATIONS

Ayatsport, Capital of the World 10
Warrior arrives at the Palace of Parliament 15
The Families of Ayat and Nya 36
"The Flying Pig" 73
Merry's Escape 127
The Children of the Plague 142
"Freedom Home" 174
Departure from Eldry 207
Gift from a Stranger 218

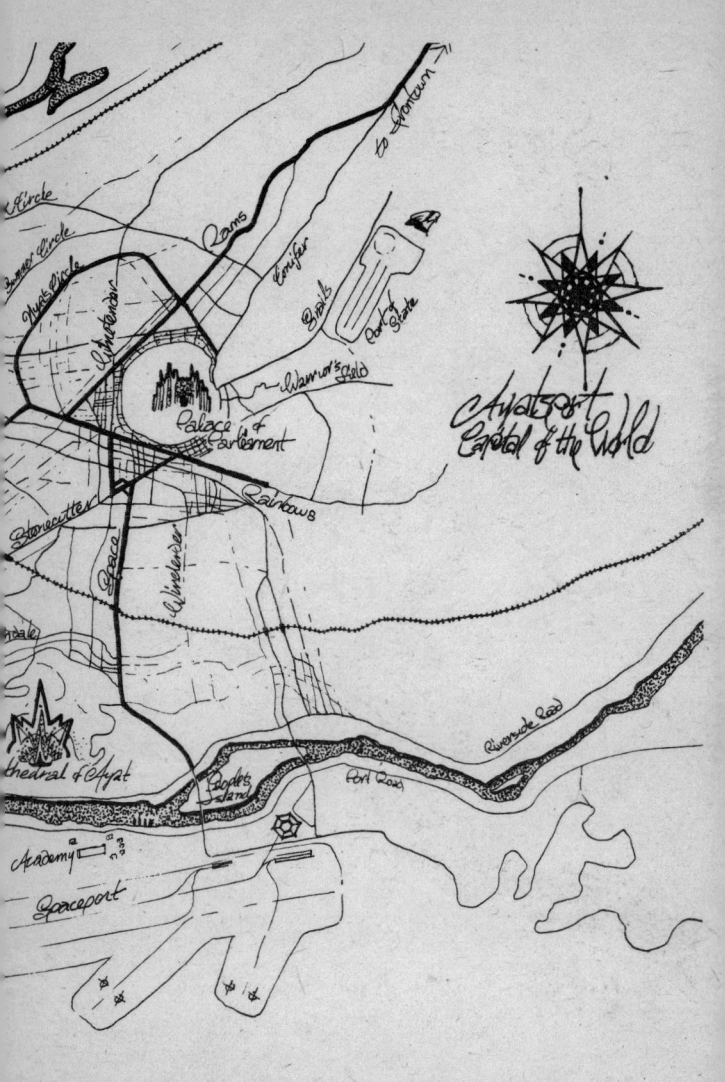

CHAPTER ONE

At Ayat's Tree

The Palace of Parliament at Ayatsport is a petrified thicket which looms from the summit of a conical hill in the Garden of Gods. The turrets and spires resemble tree trunks, and the Palace facade—carved from onyx, obsidian and black marble—writhes with vines, thorn brambles, and garlands of all the flowers of the World.

As Ayat sets, his rays strike the surviving flecks of a gold foil that once encased the sculptured leaves and blossoms, and the building seems to light itself from within with a red flame. When Nya brightens the night, creatures within the vines and brambles seem to awaken, yawn, open blue-green eyes; by nightsun, the thicket bloats as if intending to send out tendrils to eat the air over the world.

Historians dispute the commencement and completion years of the structure; most date it from "late in the Age of Artisans." From an earlier, but equally uncertain date, is the tree of high-purity gold which stands at the base of the conical hill—Ayat's Tree.

The Tree of Gold, say theologians, was placed by Ayat himself; and it is from the branches of it that the principle of life emanates.

For millennia—through the reigns of Kinbi, Nei and Bastonetu; the Age of Artisans; the Age of Awakening; the Age of Mechanisms; the Age of War; and through all the turmoil of Unification—the Tree produced its own defense through superstition. But now the lower branches are denuded, and only the upper half remains to be protected by the unsightly electrified fence (erected some thirty years ago) and the omnipresent Palace Police.

The first leaf to be stolen was taken only about seventy-five years ago—by an old woman named Agate Brickman. She, and the children the leaf would have fed, were ceremonially buried alive.

It is said that superstition has failed because the Gods are losing their power. But do not the suns still shine? Some have dared say the Gods were never more than myth, that mankind is maturing. Scientists are the enemy, cry the priests: they give us telescopes and space ships that violate the domain of the Gods, and that cripple faith. Politicians temporize with the notion that all failure stems from the helplessness of the masses. And the people attempt to believe all these things, and none of them. This is why our recent Revolution seems to have changed both everything and nothing.

It is ironic that a culture based from the beginning of time on an unquestioned worship of physical nature is oblivious to the existence of seeds—when those seeds are within the mind. The Revolution was planted, not five years ago when animosities bloomed, but when mankind emerged from the caves—no, from the seas. The Revolution was but a way-stop along our striving for life.

This narrative, however, confines itself to the ideas and events—previously known to precious few—of the new Revolution, the outbreak of hostility sometimes called the Ky Rebellion.

With the planet-wide census of this year, a poll taken reveals that nearly eighty percent of World's population is unaware, even, that a war was waged. This book is addressed to that majority for whom an extraterrestrial battle is no battle at all, a mere score of deaths fails to constitute a military casualty, an enemy a year away is no enemy; and for whom ideas do not exist.

It began on a typical overcast day of early autumn—the fifth day of the seventh month of the year 4110 (Calendar of the Gods).

It began with preparations for a parade, when the Garden and the streets of Ayatsport swarmed with

citizens anticipating a break in the monotony of days. Mallets were poised over drums. Hands rested ready on the valves of trumpets.

A space freighter, *Watchful Monz*, presumed lost, had been sighted and was approaching to land; and nothing prompts ceremony like heroes risen from the dead. Additionally, the freighter was believed to be brimmed with badly needed mechanical and electronic parts, radioactive minerals needed by power stations Worldwide, and other items of trade from Ky Colony.

The largest mass of spectators stood or sat on the mossy slopes within the Garden facing the tunnel opening near the base of Ayat's Tree—the fountainhead of the parade. They became restless with the rising of Nya, who lent blue to the residual amber of departed Ayat and made the overcast a pallid yellow-green. They huddled closer together; their talk created a sound like that of wind through caverns.

A crocus plane, its body a receptacle and its rotors a fan of petals, came to hover over Ayat's Tree. The mechanical bud dropped a strand, as if to begin a web, and from it dangled a space pilot in familiar forest green.

Attempting to identify him, the crowd issued a tentative cheer, as much from impatience as interest.

CHAPTER TWO

Isle Firemaker

The man dangling there on the brink of celebrity was Friend Warrior, a space pilot whose name was better known than his appearance. He had thrice made the Syrdo journey, the last time as commander of *Syrdo's Children*, and had captured public attention by his successful experiment to transplant World seeds into Syrdo soil—albeit in a greenhouse on the forbidding planet.

Friend Warrior was an orphan raised by the state, a man wholly aware of his advantages over orphans raised by the street. He was a sterling example of state ideals; he knew it and, out of gratitude, endeavored to keep himself that way.

He trembled as he descended gripping the unwinding strand, not from fear of height or falling, nor from knowing he was watched by thousands; he was excited because he was about to meet his personal champion. Consonant with his philosophy of gratitude, his champpion was everyone's champion—Isle Firemaker. Friend had read every book about the venerable paragon of our century of peace. Isle Firemaker was as much his hobby as his hero.

Isle Firemaker's early life was legend, but more believable to school children than arithmetic. This was the man who, as a boy, was imprisoned for stealing milk for his ailing mother; who insisted he serve an extra year while true penance permeated his soul; who discovered in prison the despotism of the mayor of his mountain village; who exposed the despot and won as his reward admittance into the Academy of Engineers; who earned acceptance for space pilot training; and who then volunteered for the most dangerous mission available.

From Pitman's fourteenth-grade history of the Presidency of Lake Groomsman:

> Nine cadets on a training mission were marooned when their starboard attitude booster (fueled with a primitive solid propellant) exploded. Ground-based radio heard screams, then silence. Isle Firemaker insisted a rescue attempt be made, and he volunteered to lead it.
>
> In the hostile blackness of space, with the great ball of World turning slowly, streaked with blue and white, and with the Gods Ayat, Nya and Monz visible and watchful, the four would-be rescuers located the derelict and found a vast rent in the side of the cabin. Inside were the bodies of six unsuited men, but no sign of the other three—whose suits and helmets were also missing.
>
> They are alive, dying of loneliness and fear in the void, said Firemaker.
>
> Further complicating the search, Monz had recently emitted three successive flares from his distant red-glowing fire; radio communication was difficult, at times impossible. The cadets under Firemaker's command laughed when they saw him attempting to locate the men with optical instruments alone; but Firemaker found them.
>
> Alone with a back-jet, Firemaker retrieved Reason Bronzeman—at death's very door—who explained that he and two others had been outside effecting repairs when the explosion hurled them away. Another point of drifting light turned out to be Dean Priest, dead, his suit torn in the blast. And he spotted the third cadet, Wisdom Steward, at a distance beyond the safe capacity of the back-jet Firemaker carried. Nevertheless, he sped with measured bursts of power toward the helpless man.
>
> Steward was alive but raving with terror. He attacked the brave Firemaker and wrenched the back-jet from its clamps, and pushed Firemaker, tumbling, away.
>
> In his panic, Steward overused the back-jet, missed the rescue ship, and was lost. Unable to find either Steward or Firemaker, the rescue party returned to World.
>
> A week later, ground stations received an impossible message from a transmitter that had not been used in eighteen years. The message was, "I'd like to come home, now. Firemaker."

Finding himself drifting roughly toward an old orbital station, Firemaker had punctured his own suit to create the faint propellant he needed to allow him to reach it. Inside he found enough oxygen to pressurize a cabin or two, and enough dried food for the work ahead of him: rejuvenating the transmission equipment.

Only a year following that incident, Firemaker was selected to be among those to ferry the heaviest load ever amassed for delivery to Ky: six thousand tons of power tools and building materials. The ten astronauts involved in the seven-year mission were instructed to spend their three years on Ky in whatever manner suited their pleasures. According to the same Academy text quoted previously:

> Firemaker found that many of the original colonists had either perished or undergone profound changes, that now they and their descendants had become hard-working, productive and ingenious people. He fell in with them, aided them in the application of the new tools and materials, and helped found the planet's principle city, Nyasport. While there, he married Peace Gardner, who died bearing him a daughter.

That was fifty years ago, when Firemaker was but thirty. He returned to World on his appointed flight, leaving his new-born daughter with relatives of his wife. But thereafter he kept himself on perpetual standby to make the grueling expedition to Ky Colony. With the advent of the staging depots on Syrdo—Ayat's intermediary planet—and on Ru—Nya's intermediary—Firemaker became one of the very few regularly to visit the distant Colony itself.

One such mission, twenty-one years prior to the date of the parade to honor the arrival of *Watchful Monz*, insured Firemaker a place among the Gods. Having already won every prize, award and medallion offered by World Government, he was, following this event, made an honorary Member of Parliament. He still bears the only such status conferred in our history.

The event is known to the public as the Ky Plague; but until very recently, its nature has remained a state secret. The following is an excerpt from a document held in the palace records. It was received from a physician at Ky:

The first incidence of the disease was minor and occurred sixteen months ago [remember that a Ky year is only fourteen months long, as opposed to World's twenty]. We found no cure, and seven-fifteenths of the victims perished. Seven months later there was another, larger outbreak, in which nearly two thousand died. Now, at the incidence of our third outbreak, it is clear that the trouble is cyclical and increasing in scope.

Our scientists have determined that the disease is caused by two micro-organisms in concert; and a preventive innoculation has been devised. But our supplies are exhausted, and we cannot manufacture the serum in quantity locally. The complete formulae follow. We need supplies from World as soon as is humanly possible. It is doubtful that I will be here to assist when your mission arrives; for I myself have contracted the disease.

Ky was at that time practically as distant from World as it can be. Via established orbits, utilizing the best engines then in existence, the trip was certain to take almost two years. From the Unity World Encyclopaedia:

When Isle Firemaker learned that his daughter [now married with a four-year-old son] had not yet been afflicted, he, it is said, slept for a week in the corridors of the Palace waiting to present his plan for aid to Ky.

The plan met with disapproval at first; it seemed too dangerous and too expensive for the people of World. He requested assembly of a ship in orbit, one so laden with propellant that a path requiring almost constant acceleration could be undertaken. Ultimately the hero was granted his ship, which he named *Swift Eldry*. He undertook the ten-month mission alone so as not to add weight to the vessel and not to endanger others.

He found, on Ky, a frightened and fragmented society, suffering, he said, "as much from isolation as from disease." The hero's daughter and son-in-law had by then perished, and his grandson was being cared for on a farm the plague had not reached. Firemaker, it is said, frequently risked life and limb to carry the serum to outlying districts. "He acted," a Ky reporter opined, "as if he had no concern for his own welfare." Asked later about the remark, Firemaker confirmed, "I suppose that's true. My daughter had died." Three years later, Firemaker returned to World, to a week of parades and festivities.

Firemaker's most recent journey was unique in the annals of space travel; it was a pleasure jaunt, his retirement gift from a grateful World. Firemaker merely wanted to grant a request from his grandson, Forest Singer, now a young man. Forest asked to be sent a tutor—an historian of some reputation on World—and suggested that Firemaker and the tutor bring with them a group of bright World youngsters who might study the ways of the Colony in preparation for diplomatic and sociological service. This, through World's gift, Firemaker was able to do. (Four years later, only two of the eight students, Sky Tinsmith and Merry Weaver, returned with Firemaker; the others elected to remain to become Colonials.)

These were among the facts floating near the surface of Friend Warrior's mind, the facts charging his nerves and emotions, as he descended the crocus strand, saluted Ayat's Tree, then dropped to the ground at the mouth of the Palace tunnel.

Prior to the Age of Mechanisms, mounted horror spewed forth from these Palace tunnels, in the terrifying uniforms of State Patrols. Since Unity, however, the underground stables have sheltered only ceremonial steeds—creatures so pampered and lazy that their inept leathery wings are left attached for decoration.

Warrior ran, his boots banging against the granite floor, into the reverberant vaulted chamber of the Palace stables.

Noticing eyes turned toward him, he slowed to a more respectful walk as he approached Stone Lightman, the President of the World. He said, "Sir, I have come from the Spaceport, where the approach of *Monz* has been calculated."

The President smiled faintly and asked him, "Why have they sent so unconventional a messenger?"

This was not the question Warrior expected. He stammered, "I—the Controller felt that I might bring a message as swiftly by crocus as it could be sent down by radio and runner from the Palace above. I—they—he also felt that I might be added to the parade roster."

The President nodded; he understood too much. "That's enterprising," he said, "of someone. Then the

Controller believes *Monz* will land safely?"

"Yes, sir."

"The estimated landing time?"

"In about three hours; 26:05."

The President was momentarily thoughtful, shrugged, and said, "Ride beside and slightly behind Firemaker."

"Thank you, sir."

Mental blinders had kept Friend Warrior's eyes solely on President Lightman. Now his eyes panned the stables almost too swiftly for him to see anything.

His eyes found a man who seemed to be walking through the heat of a spotlight—though the stable was uniformly lighted; who seemed extraordinarily tall—though he was but a few centimeters taller than Warrior; who seemed massively built—though this was due to his silver ceremonial armor; whose white hair seemed incandescent, mouth seemed a carving of justice, and eyes seemed omniscient—though they were only amused and clear, with gray irises. Isle Firemaker was walking directly, deliberately, toward Warrior.

"Has the Spaceport received any radio messages from *Monz*?" the legend asked, his voice soft but firm.

"No, Firemaker," Warrior answered, barely breathing. "We assume their radio is out."

"And no word from Ky?"

"No, sir. In fact—"

"You wonder about the Colony's radio silence of recent months?"

"Yes. There's speculation."

"There's speculation at the Palace, too."

Warrior's gaze flitted among the ruby "berries" and silver "leaves" of the hero's breastplate.

Firemaker said, "The Colonists have refused any further commerce or communication until we agree to regard them an independent state."

Warrior's eyes widened. "You're afraid the *Monz*—?"

"We must not show surprise at anything we find when we reach the Spaceport." Firemaker said lightly to the President: "This parade is a serious mistake."

"Nevertheless," President Lightman said dryly, "I hope you enjoy it."

Firemaker quickly donned the remainder of his hero's garb, and Warrior stood still for a bedecking; yellow garlands were draped over his astronaut's green.

"What is your name?" Firemaker asked as the two approached their horses.

"Friend Warrior, sir."

"Have you ridden a winged steed before, Friend?"

"No, sir."

The hero agilely hiked himself into the small antique saddle. "There's a gimmick to it, that adds a touch of mystery. Notice—my legs almost touch the leading edges of the wing-shoulders. You can guide the animal by nudging him there, leaving your hands uninvolved. Push back against the right wing, and the animal will turn to the right. Left—to the left. Also, if you can learn to ride with both legs always lightly touching the wings, the beast will keep his wings extended. He looks more mythological that way."

Riding toward the stable doors, Warrior tried it; it worked. He heard the flap of leather and looked back to see the creature's wings stretched full out.

Firemaker laughed. "Another thing. As we pass beneath major archways on the route, flocks of white bats will be released."

"Yes, sir, I've seen—"

"What you may not have noticed is that they tend to drop a clear, smelly excrement. When they do, you continue to smile and wave and salute as if nothing has landed in your hair, on your shoulder, in your eye. That is the essence of heroism."

Warrior tried to keep his response to a smile, but it burst into a laugh. He knew with utmost certainty that bat excrement had nothing to do with the heroism of Isle Firemaker.

They waited for the signal to begin. Friend stared unconsciously at Firemaker and was startled and embarrassed when Firemaker smiled and asked, "Do you have a question?"

"Oh, no sir, I—"

Firemaker faintly inclined his head. The subtle gesture had the mesmerizing effect of demanding: Ask it.

"I've wondered, always wondered—when you were a boy, why did you ask for that additional year of imprisonment?"

"I didn't."

"But all the accounts—?"

"I tried many times to submit corrected passages. Apparently they didn't care for my prose."

A trumpet deep within the chambers sounded the familiar intervals of the ages-old herald fanfare; the sound echoed in the tunnels until the separate notes blended into a chord. Warrior felt his horse, which was less ignorant of parade procedure than he, stir and shift its forelegs impatiently.

CHAPTER THREE

Incident at Retribution Square

Breath lunged into tubes tangled like ivy, past ornate pitch valves decorated with jade and gems, out along gently funneled metal to glittering enameled blossoms. Intricate combinations of octaves, fifths, and thirds mingled in the air to become all the qualities of beauty in sound—as one hundred trumpeters stepped from the tunnel beneath Ayat's Tree into the Garden of Gods. They entered a misty atmosphere in which distances were exaggerated under a thin layer of cloud lighted coolly by Nya.

Firemaker, his horse majestically flexing its wings, followed the trumpeters. Blue-gray glinted from the silver of his armor, and sparks of reddish purple leapt from the rubies on his chest.

Friend Warrior rode to his left and slightly behind him. His eyes were wide and moist and fixed on the parade route ahead.

Behind the heroes marched fifty representatives of healthy young humanity, naked but for their multi-colored garlands, who sang a counterpoint to the trumpets. Their song promised that the forthcoming generation would more nearly accomplish the will of Ayat. For many of the handsome youths and lithe maidens this was also an initiation into the adult world—their first official service to the State.

Next cavorted an offering of the animals: mimes and tumblers dressed to resemble everything from prehistoric saurians to the stub-winged pigs of every farm. A ripple of laughter followed the three new entries: a bear in the coveralls of a coal miner, an ostrich wearing a domestic's apron, and a mock vulture, its wings an all-consuming cape, who wore the black bubble hat of a villain from a children's book. Drums—fashioned to represent gourds and melons—played just the right tripping syncopation for the circus antics of the animals.

Thus constituted, the parade passed the perimeter of the Garden and turned south under the Victory Arch— the first of six massive stone, almost prehistoric arches along the way.

Under the arch, trumpets and drums joined in ascending arpeggios; snowy bats rose like placards defying gravity; and the crowd, so tightly packed it formed a new pavement for the streets extending in all directions, uttered a deep-throated, satisfied cheer.

Heading south down Winetender, the parade collected entries assembled elsewhere; these were dignitaries— mayors of buroughs, secretaries of commodity ministries, neighborhood monitors and the like—who rode in open vehicles patterned on the streamlined denizens of the nine seas. Ordinary citizens invited to join in formed, behind the dignitaries, the walking kite-tail of the parade.

Under the Brotherhood Arch at the Boulevard of Rainbows... the Arch of Renunciation at the Circle of Toads... into the square at Winetender and Stonecutter, a major commercial center, toward the Arch of Retribution....

The elder knight signaled for Warrior to pull closer to him. "How do you like parading?" he shouted.

"They call out my name!" Warrior said.

"They've been told who you are, and word travels faster than our horses."

Retribution square was well lighted—both by nightsun and by the mercury-vapor lamps on spindly towers of the central sculptured garden. The buildings fronting the square were the same as those standing today: the massive, irregular brick pyramids, matted with ivy, which were the dormitories for unmarried laborers; the newer concrete tower, decorated with carvings of animals, which housed many of this district's families; numerous shops—a clothing exchange, food shops, a pharmacy, two cafeterias, numerous plant nurseries—which filled the street levels of old mansions converted to warehouses; and lording over all: the Retribution Arch—intended to look like lofty tree trunks touched at the top, but, done in the imprecise style of ancient architects, looking more like the ragged legs of some great two-legged beast which had been lopped in half at the waist. People were packed into the garden, hanging out of windows, lining the balconies of the dormitories, and flowing in the streets—making way for the approaching parade.

Firemaker and Warrior were still talking about the magic of celebrity as they made the turn onto Stonecutter, approaching the Arch.

Suddenly there was a penetrating whine, a streak of bright white light, a crackling explosion, and a din of shouts and screams from the stunned multitude.

In the next instant, Warrior had leapt from his rearing steed and pulled Firemaker to the ground.

A tiny rocket-bomb had narrowly missed Firemaker, struck the paving stones near the curb, and sent masonry shrapnel flying, stinging, wounding, and in two cases blinding.

A second shot screamed past; it lodged in a woman's back and exploded her like a melon catapulted against a wall.

Most of the crowd—yelling, mashing and trampling one another—pulled back; but a dozen or so ran toward the parade shouting Firemaker's name. Presumably they had to see that he was safe—perhaps to offer help, perhaps to shield the hero's body with their own.

"Go back!" he bellowed at them.

They gratefully obeyed; they vanished with the others into doorways and the alleys and streets between buildings.

A platoon of green-clad police appeared seemingly from nowhere and dispersed into the buildings.

One young policeman, frantic in his concern, ran to the heroes who still crouched beneath their horses. "Are you all right?"

Firemaker said sharply, "The shots came from the top of the arch."

The young man uttered something like a choked gasp, pivoted, and tore off toward the center of the park, where his superior stood like a hub within the swirling activity.

The Square became deathly quiet.

In time, a policeman silhouetted against blue at the top of the Arch yelled down: "All clear! Nothing here but cages of bats! The batkeepers are gone!"

At that Firemaker got to his feet. Warrior nodded and rose; he offered to help Firemaker mount and was rebuffed with a smile.

"I'm not that old and venerable," he said.

A megaphone-amplified voice from one of the dormitory balconies called down: "Wait until the buildings have been searched!"

Firemaker replied loudly, "Let the parade continue."

As if the Gods wished to support him, to stress that no more time should be lost, the awesome roar of rocket fire began to rattle the air.

Cautiously, spectators made their way back onto the streets, their eyes skyward.

The overcast seemed to catch fire a few seconds before *Watchful Monz* burned a hole in it. The space-worthy whale rode down on a sphere of blinding plasma, a minor deity that displaced more air than a billion thunderbolts. The ground began to vibrate as if machinery were at work beneath it. Some observers fell to their knees prayerfully; others stood transfixed; many shed tears of thanksgiving because the Gods had brought the lost adventurers home again.

Before the rumbling diminished, the corps of trumpets joined it sending their song of triumph to the sky. The parade resumed at a faster rate and filed under the Arch and onto the Boulevard of Space—from which intersection the paraders saw the man-made God briefly brighten the spires of Ayat's Cathedral before settling gently toward the ground beyond People's Island. Then the world was blue again, and quiet except for the trumpets and drums and cheering.

CHAPTER FOUR

The Fate Of
WATCHFUL MONZ

"The parade is not to pass," an official of the Spaceport told Firemaker; "but it is requested that you, the Prefect, the Mayor of the South Borough, and the wife of the Ky Ambassador—she's riding with the Mayor—be admitted."

Some trumpeters and youths heard this and relayed the rumor that something was wrong.

"Have the...survivors disembarked?" Firemaker asked the official as the select group was issued through the gate.

The official stared at Firemaker, wondering at his prescience. "Yes sir; they're on the service train."

"The cargo?"

"There is no cargo."

The terminal building was architecturally rendered so as to resemble a bee hive. Errand boys and girls made echoing clacks as they ran across the hexagonal granite tiles of the terminal floor. An announce system was frantically intoning: "Assistant controllers Wheelturner, Miller, and Mason—report to the central complex at once...." As Firemaker's party approached a group of officials who must have been flown in by crocus from the Palace, the shuttle train entered the building with a descending electric whine and pulled to a stop at the hexagonal platform at the west end of the building.

Firemaker softly asked his guide, "Is Ambassador Harvester on the train?"

"Yes, sir."

"Is he alive?"

"Yes."

Firemaker took the hand of the Ambassador's wife. He said to the group, "With your permission," including no question mark in his intonation, and led the woman up the steps to the platform. The train's automatic doors slid back, but no one emerged. A pilot standing there moved aside to allow Firemaker and the woman to enter.

A crew of sixteen had left World for a rendezvous with Ky merchants on Syrdo. Seven had returned. One wore an eye patch; another lay on a stretcher, both his legs missing; two had lost their right arms. One of those two was the Ambassador.

Harvester saw his wife. In slow animation, his face lost lines of worry and tears welled in his eyes. "It doesn't hurt," he whispered through smiling lips as he folded his good arm around her. Sobbing, she squeezed him tightly, wordlessly. Her name was Meadow.

"May I be excused?" the Ambassador asked Firemaker.

"Of course. Three Foxes at midnight?"

Harvester nodded as the pair walked, still embracing, out into the terminal.

CHAPTER FIVE

At The Inn Of Three Foxes

The official report of the Ayatsport Press held that the crew of *Watchful Monz* had encountered mechanical trouble and natural disasters while negotiating their landing at the Syrdo staging depot; therefore no cargo had been accessible to them. An illicit publication, however, speculated that World merchant spacemen had been attacked by hostile Ky forces. It may be that a servant or hostess at the Inn of Three Foxes smuggled out scraps of information overheard from the midnight conversation of Isle Firemaker and Sagacious Harvester.

The Inn was situated (it has since been shut by North Borough Police) on a side street not far from Palace Circle, in a dilapidated neighborhood. It was not frequented by politicians because it was considered both too dangerous and too common; consequently it was generally overlooked by spies and gossips. Illegal drugs and drinks were sold in a barroom, the decor of which placed it in the wilds of an arctic forest; ornaments featured copulating creatures and ludicrous representations of religious rites involving wildlife. In a back room black as a coal mine, men and women danced naked; and private cubicles were available for casual sex. It was in one of these small rooms that the two leaders of men met.

They sat on log benches at a cyprus-stump table, under a dangling orange light bulb. Firemaker's first question was presumptive: "Are they prepared to wage war?"

"You know the Colonists; they think they are prepared for anything. They expect to have to defend themselves—against our inevitable attack."

"What happened on Syrdo?"

"Haven't you spoken with your grandson since the event?"

"Once, but I was able to learn only that he was not pleased by what happened at Syrdo. One cannot speak confidentially in a broadcast. I hoped Forest might have found a way to send me a letter."

"I suppose I am that letter. Do you know why I was on Syrdo?"

"Had you been exiled?"

Harvester nodded. "Between us, it was a friendly exile. I have no enemies at Ky, and I see the logic of their breaking ties with World Government. Furthermore, I was happy to come home. Meadow had returned a year earlier for reasons of health, and I was anxious to be with her. Firemaker, they have succeeded! They have abolished all forms of government—'organized coercion,' they call it—on their planet. The last tax was dropped three years ago, and their last politician abdicated a few weeks before I was... respectfully asked to leave."

"Tell me about the attack."

"There was friction from the moment of landing. Nonverbal resentment—the sort that builds. Forest personally greeted the *Monz* crew. Do you know that your grandson has become quite a respected leader at the Colony?"

"I'm not surprised. Go on."

"I'm afraid no one took him seriously when he set forth the terms his men had come to offer. He insisted that before any goods changed hands, the chief pilot of *Monz*, Stone Carpenter, had to obtain official assurance from World that thenceforward no power would be exercised over the citizens of Ky. Our Government being so closemouthed, this was the first the *Monz* crew had heard of our position."

"Our? You consider yourself a Colonist in this?"

Harvester smiled sheepishly. "Only in my child-like soul. My head knows their anarchy will fail, so my allegiance is with World, as always."

"Carpenter refused to make the call?"

"He laughed. I'm afraid he regarded your rebel relative as some kind of madman. He took it upon himself to send no message and to threaten that the cargo would be taken by force unless the Ky team came to its senses."

"So Ky men took the initiative and attacked first?"

"Yes. By that time I had been transferred to the *Monz*. It wasn't night, of course, since in springtime there is no night on that crazy planet. Ayat does a little jig in the southern sky while Nya bobs in the north and Monz zips uselessly from horizon to horizon. But it was a night hour. Only a few of us were aboard the ship; most were in the recreation hall of the depot building. I was settling myself into my new cabin, strapping books onto a shelf, as I recall, when there was an explosion of such force that I could feel its vibrations through the metal of the shelf. That, I later learned, was the blast which wiped out the ship's radio and several other instruments."

"Was Forest—?"

"Oh, he tried to talk them out of doing anything. I thought he had succeeded. I'm sure he had nothing to do with the attack; he may not even have known about it until afterward."

"Go on."

"Everyone made fatal mistakes that night. I made mine by fleeing the ship, fearing an explosion of propellant. There was only one way to run—through the telescoping airlock joining us to the depot. With stupid disregard for caution, four of us poured into the building—where we were immediately cut down by explosive bullets.

"When the smoke cleared, I was stunned; and one of my arms was missing. There were several from the *Monz* crew near me, and I screamed that we had to return to the ship. We were doing just that when another explosion jolted the depot. There was that terrifying sound of wind, where no such sound belonged. We barely got out before a wall blew out. For all practical purposes, Firemaker, there is no longer an outpost building on Syrdo!

"It seems only minutes later that I was aware of the Ky ship's departure; but then I was only half conscious. We still had our timetable; our guidance system and engines worked; so at the appointed time, we lifted off and set our course for World."

"What do you think will happen next?"

"I don't know. Perhaps nothing, if we allow Ky to strike its own course."

"You know that can't happen, not after the thousands of years it took us to unify the World. It would be like allowing children who've thrown tantrums to thereafter have their own way in everything."

"I know."

"Do you feel that the attack on the *Monz* was premeditated."

"No, I seriously doubt it."

"You've heard about the attempt to assassinate me today?"

"Meadow told me. I'd love to hear your—"

"Was that the work of underground Colonial sympathizers here?"

"Surely not! What would that gain them?"

"Respect, of sorts. Acknowledgment that they are earnest, and powerful—to be feared."

"But that's not the image they want for themselves! They really mean World no harm; they just want to be left alone."

"How much of your story do you believe we should take to the people?"

Harvester laughed. "You're testing me, my old friend; and I'll answer you honestly. I'd like to tell them everything. Of course, I'd be buried alive if I did; so I won't."

Firemaker smiled and rested his hand over Harvester's. "No one will learn your secret from me," he said warmly, amused.

"And you? How stands the World's most celebrated hero—deep in his soul? Aside for your concern for Forest, where will your ideas take you?"

Firemaker shrugged with his white bushy eyebrows and said, "I don't know... quite frankly, I don't know."

CHAPTER SIX

How The Gods Came To The Cathedral of Ayat

It is said that in the time before, Ayat dwelled alone and lonely in a castle he had fashioned of fire. He contemplated the only thing he knew: himself. He was childhood.

Monz was restlessness, a wanderer in search of a hearth, who befriended the God of Light and told him of woman.

"Bring her to me," Ayat commanded. And Monz traveled to far dimensions to find a mate for his new master. (*The Odyssey of Monz* is the most ancient of testaments, adapted from prehistoric tablets.)

Monz discovered Nya—lovely beyond light, puissant but lacking one gift: the ability to distort the truth. She was simplicity.

And in this she became disillusionment as Monz became profligacy. On their journey to Ayat, the Goddess and the Wanderer knew physical love. Seeing into Ayat's innocent and impassioned soul, she confessed it.

Banished but now able to love no other save Ayat, Nya called to her the deities Wit, Grace and Beauty—called La, Ky, and Ru—and created her own cool castle on the frontier of Ayat's influence. She kept her spirit in patience for seven eternities (one for each planet, no doubt, thus giving us our superstitious number).

Monz fled, weeping—the first bearer of guilt.

Ayat softened yet indulged in stubborn pride. He devised Eldry, messenger of love, to woo the Goddess on his behalf; but, mindful of the perfidy of Monz, Ayat castrated his messenger. Appalled by Ayat's barbarism, Nya refused to reply to the repeated entreaties carried by Eldry.

Monz, his loyalty to Ayat and Nya having become obsessive, returned treasure-laden. His gifts were the Seeds of Life, and with them Ayat fashioned the World (first chapter, *The Book of Ayat*). He sculpted a realm of majesty and promise and populated it with Humankind, whom he charged with the tasks of maintenance and beautification. He presented the World to Nya as a gift of love and repentance; it was to be their Paradise in which their eternal happiness would be consummated.

"When on all the World there is no imperfection, no injustice, and when the beauty of it surpasses my own imagination, I will be yours," the Goddess promised.

To insure perfectability, Ayat called upon Syrdo the Philosopher, who prescribed Man's life, made of him a gardener and caretaker, and forbade him the enterprises of murder, theft, cruelty, dishonesty, and greed; for these were deemed in discord with the purpose of Life: cooperatively to make a Paradise for the Gods. With Ayat's blessing, Syrdo provided that, "when after millenia of suffering Man has accomplished his task, he will be granted freedom from pain, accessibility to all pleasure, and life everlasting. He will be invited to dwell in the Paradise he has made, among the Gods."

But Man, intent upon self-gratification, denied the omnipotence of Ayat and the wisdom of Syrdo. The World became overgrown with weeds and strewn with decay. Monz grew red with fury, and his flares of white sent one hundred days of lightning and fire to sear the face of the decadent World; and Syrdo asked Ayat to strip Man of the power of flight. Man descended from the skies to the level of the sluggish beasts of the field (see *The Fall of Man*).

Thus condemned to a joyless life of toil and inferiority, Man subsisted for thousands of years expending his energies on bare survival and suffering the Guilt of Monz for neglecting Ayat's purpose. The priests of antiquity studied the heavens and interpreted the movements of the Gods. When Ayat and Nya traveled close, summer and happiness fell upon World; when Monz flared white, a season of repentance was declared; when Ayat lighted the day and Nya the night, winter and hardship approached as the Gods expressed their impatience with Man. For thousands upon thousands of years.

Modern creative Man was born in the year 3749 (Calendar of the Gods) when World was fragmented into hostile nations, hostile tribes, when the man we today call Friend Inventor felt he could alleviate the approaching blindness afflicting King Bastonetu. Friend Inventor was a fabricator of glass who had noted the material's property of distortion.

After providing spectacles for the King, he constructed a telescope with which he looked into the heavens, into the faces of the Gods. In the year 3749.

For suggesting that Ayat, Nya and Monz were insensate balls of flame—and that the moralist Syrdo, the watchdog Nxo, the messenger Eldry, and Nya's art-producing handmaidens, were merely worlds like our own—Friend Inventor was ceremonially executed. (It is widely believed that his body was the first to be used deliberately to fertilize; he lies beneath the tallest ironwood grove in the Garden of Ru at Stormsville). But in secret, his son, Morninglight Inventor, carried on the work; and at the time of his natural death, he left posterity a theory of gravitation, and a suggestion that Nya's planet Ky was water-covered.

Being atheist, the ideas of Friend and Morninglight Inventor traveled but furtively—until the year 3911, when the courageous theologian, Blessed Priest, published his *Origins*.

Of course the Gods' castles are suns, *Origins* tells us; but the benevolent Gods yet call them home. Yes, their creations are planets—metaphors set in the heavens to lead us toward an ever-bettering life. A theory of gravitation detracts naught from the power of the Gods; on the contrary, it may be their greatest invention. Furthermore (and in this, *Origins* released the mind of Man), Nya, by personifying honesty, urges Humankind to seek knowledge—even to question the structure of the Universe.

Through *Origins*' system of gentle fallacy, truth was set free. What followed was the epoch we call The Age of Awakening.

With the coming of steel, structural concrete and other

astonishing methods and materials, the first great edifices to be constructed—once Worldwide religious wars were behind us—were the Cathedrals. One of the earliest and still most imposing was the Cathedral of Ayat at Ayatsport. Its erection consumed twenty-four years and the oft-unwilling labor of many thousands; it was completed in 4002, the ninth year of Unity, the very year that an experimental missile first sped beyond the gravity of World.

A new era is coming. Future historians may grandiosely call it The Age of Freedom, or perhaps The Age of Man; and it seems both fitting and paradoxical that Ayat's Cathedral should have provided a springboard for it.

Think of beliefs as breezes, historical momentum as a wind, discontent as a pressure, and genius as a magnet for ideas. Over Ayatsport in 4110 a silent and invisible hurricane raged; in it swirled all the ideas of Humankind. The undetected maelstrom funneled to a place which called to it—in the Cathedral.

The thoughts of ages past and ages yet to come descended past the spires that made of the Cathedral a sculptured sun, and into the great Rotunda of Prayer where garlanded priests and citizens with seedlings congregated somberly, unaware of the destructive force swirling around them. Thence to subterranean levels, the other-dimensional tornado whirled unnoticed through classrooms at the College of Theology, where it weakened the half-truths of *Origins* ... down through dormitories, kitchens, private chapels, offices for administration and maintenance; down, down to the level where pumps, ventilators and generators—the internal organs—keep vital fluids flowing through the house of the Gods. Here, also, are abandoned chambers, reliquaries of dead and obsolete machinery deemed too heavy and too costly to remove. In one of these deep chambers, on the morning following the tragic arrival of *Watchful Monz*, a revolutionary worked alone by batterylight at a hand-operated printing press.

We have had occasion to mention him before, in passing. He, with Merry Weaver, returned to World with Firemaker after being educated on Ky. His name was Sky Tinsmith.

CHAPTER SEVEN

Sky Tinsmith, Infidel

The air being stuffy, he had removed his postulant's vestment and wore only body clothes; he was vulnerably slight of frame. His face, in the harsh light, was pale; in the privacy of his eyes he looked boyish, excited, unafraid; his mouth—through which he met his fellow man—made him look wounded and determined.

His work space was bright, but the illumination quickly diminished as it was sponged up by the dark fungus-covered walls and the rusty mounds of antique generators. On a stone in the wall near where he worked there was scratched a symbol:

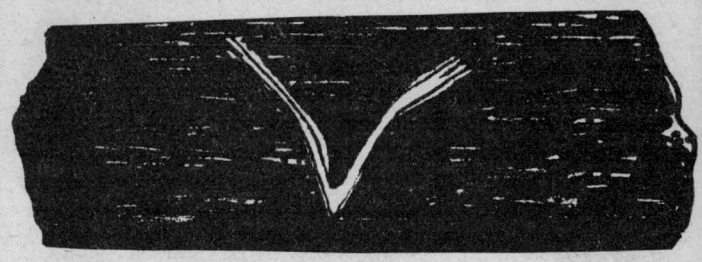

Two-thirds of a triangle, the essence of an arrow, a representation of wings in flight? Whatever the device might have meant to the secretive young philosopher, it came to mean "Infidel" to the World and Ky. It was with this symbol alone that Sky Tinsmith signed his iniquitous papers.

That morning he was duplicating an essay on

happiness, which contained these inflammatory words:

"To suggest that the Gods expect toil and self-denial of Man, while it is clear to all that the crux of Godliness is self-satisfaction, is an absurdity. To suggest that the Gods, whose stories exemplify freedom, support Man's enslavement, is hypocrisy. For Government to deny Man, on religious grounds, the pleasures and private life we grant to the animals of the wild—this is ultimate blasphemy."

An editorial in the Ayatsport Press once speculated that a man who could pour out such vituperation as that evidenced in Infidel's writing ought to be identified by an insulting, swaggering manner, accusing slits of eyes, and a hot temper. But those personally close to Sky knew him as the gentlest of beings. It is not surprising that his fellow seminarians failed to guess his uniqueness among them. He may have been a criminal, but he would also have made a kind and understanding priest.

He stilled the press. He listened. He watched the door. There was a sound, perhaps a footfall. Another sound. He switched off his batterylight and waited. He heard the iron door of his hideaway creak open.

"Sky?" a feminine voice whispered in the pitch darkness.

"Merry?" he hazarded.

"Turn on the light." The door creaked again and clicked shut.

He knocked the light from his work table as he lunged, in the blackness, to turn it on. There in the upcast light from the fallen lamp stood Merry Weaver, laughing at his clumsiness.

She had the most beautiful yellow hair, deepest blue-green eyes, and most blemishless skin Sky had ever seen; but then, since he had first met her he had not studied the details of the appearance of any other woman. To him, her manner epitomized both grace and confidence; and her voice was the low silken one of heroines. Her body seemed a supple statue; its perfection was more than usually evident now, with her dark green shirt and slacks dripping wet.

"Don't you have a heating unit down here?" she asked

as she peeled off her soggy shirt, uncovering small shapely breasts. "Well, do you? I'd like to dry this."

He set up a radiant screen and made a chair-back into a drying rack. Why was she wet? She had made the passage through the sewers before and had always managed to find high shelves and dry gullies on which to travel. He hadn't expected her today; why had she come? But his curiosity was swamped by his relief that once more she had come to him.

"Go on with what you were doing," she insisted. She sat on the cold floor and tugged off her squishing boots. "What are you printing?"

As he handed her a sample of the finished work, he digested only flickering glances at her naked back, her breasts, her hands, her face—no more able to stare at her than he'd have been likely to stare into Ayat's flame.

After adjusting the one light to serve them both, Sky turned to the press again, cranking it more slowly than before. He had the silly fear that if he finished his work, she'd leave—perhaps vanish like a daydream.

Finishing the essay, she interrupted his printing. "You call the quality 'happiness,' but 'freedom' can substitute throughout, can't it?" She slid the copy across the floor toward Sky, as if it were a thing of no particular consequence.

"Well, the emphasis would shift. I'm saying that freedom, and the creative use of it, leads to happiness—not that they're exactly the same thing. Freedom doesn't guarantee happiness; it merely makes it possible."

"Does your theory extend to priests?"

"What do you mean?"

"You know what I mean. In your new world, are you to be allowed personal pleasures? Women?"

He moistened his lips; it was easier just to nod than to speak.

She laughed. "It might be interesting to be raped by a priest."

"Merry! I'd never—"

"You've already devoured me with those eyes that refuse to see me. Turn this way and look at me."

"I can't." But in the periphery of his sight, he sensed

that she had stretched out against the stones of the floor, that her hands were on her breasts. "I...."

"The great man of letters is at a loss for words?"

"It's... more that I must hide what I know is written on my face. I am more naked than you are."

"Shall I take off the rest?" When he made no movement or sound, the seductive tone left her voice; she said, "Funny, I always assumed that if you let yourself respond honestly, you'd prefer your own sex."

"Merry!"

"I'd think no less of you. You idolize Forest Singer. If you don't know it, you're the only one—"

"That doesn't mean—"

"Isn't that why you desire me, Sky—because I once belonged to Forest?"

Sky wanted to tell her that he'd loved her since their journey to Ky—before either of them had met Forest Singer. But he couldn't; he had hidden the fact too successfully—from himself as well as the others. Now, when he knew it was true, it would sound like a lie. Her notion was insulting; her manner was insulting; but the intimacy of the subject thrilled him to confusion.

"Ever had a sexual experience?"

He shook his head, still unable to look at her. He heard the suggestive popping of the snaps of her trousers.

"Then I'm right about you and Forest?"

"No."

She laughed, and Sky was unable to determine whether she was expressing disbelief—or something else. To ward off further intolerable talk, he recommenced printing. He stole a glance at her later and saw that she was sleeping.

His mind was a jumble of pictures. Merry and Forest arm in arm, kissing, talking. The small classroom on Ky. The "team" he used to think Merry, Forest and Sky to be. Night-long discussions, just the three of them, on matters of worldshaking importance, ideals, the future of the human race. That inexplicable time when Merry had seemed on the verge of killing Forest: "It isn't possible," Sky had heard Forest tell her. The long talk with Forest it had lasted a week, off and on, when he had learned of his new friend's atheism—an insurmountable wall between them. One thing was undoubtedly true: Sky had idolized Forest Singer; he still did, though now from an astronomical distance, both in kilometers and beliefs. Was Forest at fault for the violence on Syrdo? Sky wanted to think not; but a man who has rejected the Gods, has rejected Syrdo's moral guidance, is theoretically capable of any atrocity....

"Can they win?" Merry asked. Sky had not noticed that she was awake. "Can the Colony win their freedom?"

"Eventually," Sky enthused, relieved that she'd abandoned her previous subject. "Unless their moral anarchy—their wide-spread rejection of the Gods— makes them unworthy. Political anarchy allows for happiness, prevents enslavement by a State. It must prevail, because it is right."

"Right for the Colony, or—?"

"Right for Humankind. One day even our World Government will fall."

"And bury us beneath it?"

"Not if the Gods are with us."

"I see it more as a matter of timing—no offense to the Gods. Tell me, Sky, how do you read the events of yesterday—the landing of the *Monz* and the attempt on Firemaker's life?"

"I don't understand either of them."

"I mean, how will Government view the events; what will the people think? Will they connect the two?"

"I'm afraid so. It will look like Ky Colony is on the verge of attacking us—to the Government at least. They have yet to divulge enough to Ayatsport Press for the people to be much affected. But I suspect the people will be told some of the truth, soon. They might even be told that the perpetrator of the assassination attempt was Infidel."

"Did you do it?"

"Merry! Of course not. I have no idea who did. It will surely be considered the work of Colonial rebels; but Forest—I don't care how depraved his morals—would not have ordered his grandfather's death."

"You're assuming Forest is leading the rebellion?"

"Why else would he have been at Syrdo? Another thing: this violence only serves to intensify World's hatred, jealousy, of the Colony. And unless Forest and his people have lost their minds, that will act to their disadvantage. They don't want war. How could they win one—their million against the resources of World's billions?"

She nodded pensively, a trace of a smile on her lips. "Then violence discredits the Colony?"

"Yes, but it does more than that. It shakes confidence in existing peace-keeping forces. It's two-edged: it causes hatred to be directed toward the perpetrator and distrust toward those who should have prevented it. Violence— particularly from an unknown source—leaves the people insecure."

"You're saying that even if the Press blames the Colony for the violence, it might be World Government who loses face?"

"No matter who the Press blames, World Government will suffer."

"Sounds like a good reason for advocates of anarchy here to commit acts of violence."

"But it isn't. World Government is democratic; it can be altered by a change in the philosophy of the electorate. The chains we have to break are mental, not physical."

"So there you stand at your little printing press." She got to her feet pensively, slipping on her dry shirt. "You've given me something to think about, Infidel," she said cheerily.

"Don't call me that, not even here."

"Coward," she teased. But Sky felt, in the pit of his stomach, that to some extent she might have meant it. "Don't be so fragile," she admonished, reading his face. "Can I make a delivery for you?"

He checked his pocket watch. "It's a little early yet."

"They'll be waiting at the usual place?"

"They check it every day at the same time."

She gestured toward the stack of printed pamphlets. "Let me take them."

He bundled the lot with string, then handed her the rather heavy package. "Be careful," he said.

At the door, before signaling him to douse the light for her exit, she advised: "It's time you followed your own philosophy, Sky. Be the man you want to be." She smiled suggestively. "Take what you want."

In the dark, he heard her chillingly beautiful laughter, the creaking of the old metal door, then a silence so complete he could hear blood pulsing rapidly through his ears.

CHAPTER EIGHT

Where The Sewers Lead

The only light in the anteroom outside Sky's hidden shop was a single glowing dot over a service elevator. By this almost nonexistent illumination, Merry made her way to the grate in the floor through which she had entered. Below the grate was a metal platform with rusted steps leading to the sewage channel which runs beneath Cathedral Hill to the River of Lilies. On the platform Merry had left a fat tubular rifle—a launcher of miniature rocket-bombs—while she had visited Sky. Taking it now, being careful not to clang it against the platform or stair railings while slipping its strap over her shoulder, she descended into solid darkness.

Guided by the faint echoes of her cautious footsteps, by her highly developed sense of direction, and by intuition, she located a side channel that allowed her to backtrack toward the industrial district of the Southeast Borough, to a workman's access hole beneath the intersection of Windharp and Rushdale (where a splendid sculptured garden honors Ky, the Goddess of Grace). Here a ritual performed uncounted times before was repeated.

At precisely the fourteenth hour, there was a single reverberant rap sounded on a metal conduit. Merry answered it with another; then she saw a shaft of light from above. A courier at ground level looked down and saw a white rectangle being pushed into view at the bottom of the conduit. The courier descended to retrieve the stack of printed essays and take them for distribution;

he caught no sight or sound of the person who had delivered them.

The information underground was an informal, and illegal, institution in Ayatsport; it probably existed even before Unity, and it certainly still exists today. Sky Tinsmith did not begin it; he merely used it to advantage: it was the only publisher and distributor available to him. Those along its pipeline were easily and quickly converted to his way of thinking, however, and as of this date—6d-7m 4110—were already calling themselves his followers.

Merry retraced her steps back toward the Cathedral. She undoubtedly stopped a dozen times or more as she heard voices or footsteps other than her own; for the sewers are the black highways of derelicts and criminals. In all probability her shoes were nibbled at by vermin, and her hair curiously examined by diving bats. That she accomplished her passage without being raped, robbed or murdered, means that not once did she cry out in terror or surprise.

She passed her cut-off to the Cathedral and continued on to the river.

How did she cross the river unnoticed? There is a persistant rumor that Protector provided an underwater capsule of advanced design which granted secret access to his habitat for those in his employ. In 4112, when People's Island was raided and it was found that Protector had moved on, no such method of transport was found. But the rumor persists.

Suffice it to say that Merry Weaver did cross the river, in bright daylight, and was not observed doing so.

CHAPTER NINE

The Invisible Arm Of Parliament

During the eoncluding month of the Revolution, while Forest Singer's trial was in progress, Honor Townsman—known to be in service to Protector—was apprehended and interrogated at great length. He spoke freely, by all accounts willingly, before his puzzingly efficient escape. ("One day he was in his cell," said the story in the Press, "and the next day he simply wasn't!")

We dip liberally into the transcript of his interrogation in reconstructing the following scene.

When Merry Weaver arrived at People's Island that day, the lieutenant at the entrance to Protector's estate was this same Honor Townsman. He had been told that Merry was expected. He relieved her of her rocket-rifle, blindfolded her, and led her through hallways reputed to contain an extraordinary museum of fine art—where virtually every species of flora and fauna, extant and extinct, was replicated in jewels and precious metals.

Thence to the estate's gymnasium, to the bath house.

Had Merry not been blindfolded, she would have seen him upon entering the steamy room. He was neither young nor old, was of average height, and tended toward corpulency. His eyes stayed narrow, and his smiles were frequent. He sat, water up to his baggy chest, on the ledge of a sumptuous jade-and-ivory-lined pool.

Townsman watched Merry undress and led her to the pool steps.

"Too hot for you?" Protector asked.

"Not for someone who has spent most of two days in the sewers," she retorted. "How are you?"

He giggled helplessly. "You know. You know every sensation under my skin as I watch the most lovely creature in the World step naked into my bath!"

Protector instructed Townsman to remain until Merry's appointment was ended. (Townsman was convinced this request was more out of perversity—Protector liked an audience when he had snared a pretty girl—than from any practical consideration of security.)

With a double nod, Protector instructed Townsman to hand Merry a jar of soap.

"Are your parents well?" Protector asked her.

"As well as they deserve to be," she answered.

With such small talk they passed several minutes until Protector asked, as if this too were a minor matter, "Why did you kill that woman? Was it intentional?"

Merry smiled, satisfied; and after a pause, told her story:

"I had my father lure down the batkeepers. Fortunately there is an opening to the sewers inside the east leg of the arch, and it was down that opening that we tossed their bodies. I ascended to the top, took my station, and picked out a quail—one of the Sisters of Nya, a Holy woman. I waited until Firemaker was between us before I took my shots. I wanted to make it seem that not only has Ky tried to take our great hero from us, but out of carelessness has extinguished a lady of miracles. You don't object, I trust."

He said thoughtfully, "I suppose not, but your creativity is alarming."

"It's time you told me—why this vendetta against the Colony? I'd think you would thrive on political unrest, and if Ky wins independence, we'll certainly have chaos."

Townsman had never before heard anyone question Protector; and evidently the powerful man failed even to notice her audacity. He answered candidly, "I am a philosopher. I note trends. I foresee developments. Freedom and my sorts of enterprise cannot share the same planet. When the sales of all commodities are legal, my services compete with those of legitimate businessmen. I lose my monopolies. Bring me a proposal to ban a book, to condemn the sales of a drug, a law to prohibit any luxury or indulgence, and I will place all of my power and influence, even my moral indignation, behind it. Such laws add to my inventory. But around me, dear child, never mention anarchy! It would suffocate me." He laughed, but then added in seriousness: "Has it occurred to you that any government which attempts to prescribe nearly every action permitted its citizenry can be tolerated only so long as there are organizations such as mine capable of supplying forbidden pleasures? I keep our Government from seeming to be an absolute power. And the Government—take my word for this—knows it. Even the people know it, though they don't realize they do. I control a denounced, invisible, but necessary arm of Parliament."

Merry nodded. "Yes, that has occurred to me."

The water shattered around Protector as he got to his feet. He stepped down into the deeper part, where Merry stood leaning against the wall of the pool, her arms spread out on the top edge. "There is more to be done to discredit the Colony," he said. "Are you willing?"

"Of course. But next time, I think there should be an arrest. Otherwise it might seem that our inept World forces are being outwitted. Crime may occur, but the criminal must be caught."

"Amazing. That would be better, yes. Are you volunteering to be executed?"

"We'll find someone to take the blame."

"Blame it all on that pamphleteer; what do they call him? Infidel? Do you know who he is, by the way?"

She did not hesitate before answering, "I have no idea."

The chubby man sloshed forward and covered her small strong body with his, moaning, as if he felt unworthy to be doing what he was doing.

His paunch and his height relative to hers were problems; he had to squat and grip the pool edge to find his angle of entry. In doing so, he unintentionally jostled her blindfold loose.

Protector's passions apparently submerged any alarm he might have felt at her seeing his face. He merely sighed when, for the first time, he looked into her dazzling

51

zenith-colored eyes. If she recognized his moderately well known face, she kept her surprise to herself. In this appallingly undignified manner, Merry Weaver was initiated into the elite inner circle of the kingdom of the underworld. And she treated the honor much as she treated this sexual encounter—as if neither were of the remotest importance.

As Protector pumped and pummeled her against the jade wall, whapping the water with his ample shape, she kept an impassioned gaze not on the great man but on Honor Townsman—a younger man with a handsome face and an iron body.

Townsman was terrified. He knew he could be killed for expressing any desire for Merry, but he felt aroused to the point of dizziness. He could not leave without permission, and he dared not interrupt to ask for it.

After Protector shouted with a shock of sudden pleasure, Merry had to hold him up to keep his weakened body from slipping underwater. Only then could Townsman, his trance snapped, turn his eyes away.

The middle-aged snail crawled back onto his ledge.

Merry dried herself and dressed in the fresh clothing given her.

"Ask something of me!" the king of the outlaws pleaded.

She ignored his pathetic petition until she was standing at the door ready to leave. "I will." She added cryptically, "As soon as I'm sure."

Townsman assumed she already had a favor in mind.

CHAPTER TEN

Weaver's Inn
Of The Frog

If it can be accepted that Protector's organization was an unofficial arm of Parliament, it might be seen in the same light that private property served to keep a kind of pressure from building against World policies; it acted as a release valve.

The First Parliament after Unity did not outlaw private property, but merely made it "unnecessary." With everyone pooling resources Worldwide, Parliament proclaimed, "no one need want for food, clothing, lodging, and the spiritual dignity of successful living." Most privately owned homes and business which persisted tended to exist in partnership with Government, which held all mortgages. Since Unity, few have been able or eager to amass the capital required to purchase the neglected space or structures offered by the Land Office. One who did manage it was Rain Weaver, Merry's father.

Ownership was an obsessive idea to Rain Weaver, one his acquaintances claim stretched well back into his childhood. As a youth, he took up the arduous professions first of arctic sailor, then forester, then concrete mixer. All his earnings, paltry as they were, he converted to gold and hid away, while living off the nourishment of weeds and sleeping under the open sky. He indulged in no enduring friendships or romances—nothing that would restrict his wanderings in search of capital.

In his middle thirties he was able to buy a public house in the village of Bear Crossing. He had rightly assumed that the town was about to burgeon following the discovery of coal deposits. When the Government reasoned it had been hasty in relinquishing the now-valuable property, Weaver made a profit on its resale to the Government. This modest fortune allowed him to migrate to Ayatsport, to buy a piece of property, and finally to marry.

The East Borough of Ayatsport had been quite right to divest itself of the four-story brick structure Rain Weaver metamorphosed into the Inn of the Frog. The abandoned building was in an area few people dared to enter, much less live in. It was bounded on the east by the foul-smelling River of Reeds, the noisy and polluting crocus-engine manufactory on the north, a freight train depot on the west, and Ayatsport's atomic-electric plant on the south. The A-plant was the greatest single deterrent to tourism. No one knows precisely who first found a way to utilize nuclear material to raise steam for generators; but it has been common knowledge that many died before proper shielding was devised, and it was widely rumored that should the heating elements become unstable, an awesome all-destructive explosion might result. (Remember that at this time in our history, nearly five years ago, an atomic explosion had never occurred. Even so, fears were great.)

When it was announced that Weaver had purchased the property and intended to make of it an inn and public house, people thought he was crazy. But within a month of its opening, every room and apartment was occupied, and the pub on the lower floor had become popular. There are always those who would rather live in a hovel of their own choosing than in a dormitory assigned to them. Some of the occupants were undoubtedly fugitives; some were merely reclusive. Apparently, the dangers and pollutants were not sufficient to frighten people away; in fact it seems probable that the risks of the area were one of the reasons for the pub's popularity. It seemed daring to go there. At the Inn of the Frog, one might meet other daring people.

At the end of the first year, Rain Weaver made a terrible discovery. His success was causing him to fail. He owned the building outright, so there was nothing on a mortgage to pay to the Government. In balance of this, the Government assessed him dearly on his profits. Simple computing told him to shut down the pub at once and to limit the number of rooms he would let out. In this way, at least, his family would not starve and he could keep the building. (As a property owner, Government doles were unavailable to him. He had to buy all his family's needs.)

His daughter's schooling had to be ended, but he was able to offer her an apartment of her own, one that was partitioned off at the rear of what had been the public room. Merry had two cubicles, plumbing facilities, and her own door to the outside. That private entrance gave Merry ideas.

She campaigned for months and finally persuaded her father to make the windows of the unused upper floor light-tight and rent out those apartments *sub rosa*, keeping all profits for his family. Illegal tenants could use her private door.

Several of the unsavory men who took lodging in those windowless rooms also paid for Merry's wind-up affections as they passed through her quarters. Merry dared not refuse them, for fear they would report the Inn's illegal activities; and she was able to put a stop to it only when the Inn's finances were sound enough once more for the pub to reopen (on a smaller scale than before). Then the irregulars could come and go through the bar, via the front door. And it was probably Merry who instigated the occasional sale of illegal drugs which used to transpire in the pub—with her father raking off an agent's fee. She reentered school, and excelled.

Because of her exemplary scholarship, she was selected by her history tutor and Firemaker to be among the eight trained at Ky Colony. Just prior to her departure, she had a brief affair with a young tenant of the Inn who turned out to be a courier for Protector. Thus Protector grew interested in the activities of Rain Weaver. Protector sent a representative who demanded a monthly fee from Weaver in exchange for keeping the police away from his door. Merry convinced her father to barter the fee; and Rain agreed to perform minor services for Protector's organization on a semi-regular basis. It became a comfortable enough arrangement.

Rain Weaver and his family were never to live in luxury; but after this, they were living successfully, taking in a little more than they paid out, on a small piece of World they called their own.

When Merry returned from Ky, she seemed vastly changed. "Like a man," her little brother observed. She took complete charge of her father's business—and increased its efficiency. She promoted a closer affiliation with Protector. Once, when her father balked at an assignment for the organization, she carried it out for him. She murdered an uncooperative policeman.

What of her mother? Moss Weaver loved best those who decided things for her, and least those who created disturbances. She cooked, cleaned, and allowed her husband the use of her body. No one remembered that she had once been quite pretty. Rain tolerated her; Merry ignored her; and her adolescent son, Orchard, pitied her. She knew her family were Godless; so she stayed sufficiently moral for them all. They would long ago have been caught or killed, Moss believed, were it not for her prayers and offerings. In her mind, she was the family's greatest strength; and they were amused by her fantasy.

When Merry returned home from People's Island, the night after the *Monz* parade, she had with her a purse of gold coins, payment for a day's work—more than the Frog collected in a month.

"Save your soil, Mother," she said, breezing into the pub; "I'm safe."

Moss Weaver typically gave push to her prayers with pottings. At that moment she was planting a dwarf conifer, one of the most difficult plants to nurture in semitropic Ayatsport. Her sacred gardening tools, prayer seeds, and a plastic bag of dirt were arrayed on the bar before her. Behind her, the wall looked like an indoor botanic garden.

"You've been gone so long!" Moss wailed.

Disappearing into her apartment, Merry called back, "I'm going to sleep for an hour or two. Wake me for supper." The door slammed shut behind her.

Moss went on with her prayer and potting, stopping now and again to wait on a customer.

When the family ate together they had their meals at a large sycamore table in the public room. They would take turns with any customers who happened to be there at mealtime. That evening, as usual, Moss stood and loudly cried the Contrition, shedding a tear or two:

"All-giving Ayat, forgive us our destruction of these thy seeds and animals; grant us the nourishment of these paltry few organisms which we pledge to replenish manyfold during the lives you have given us."

"What did you kill today, Mother?" Merry asked. "A couple of carrots?"

"A butcher stilled the lives of the squirrels we have on our plates; we are as guilty as he."

Rain snorted an unhappy laugh. "I'm sure you and the butcher will be forgiven. Pass the mushrooms, will you, Orchard?"

The boy complied silently.

"Did you have a nice day, Merry?" her mother asked.

"Profitable. Can you say as much?" Seeing her mother's hurt expression, Merry continued, "Oh, I'm sorry, we all know you save us the fee of a housekeeper."

Rain slammed his spoon against the table. "Don't treat your mother like that!" he snarled.

Moss said, "Be quiet, Rain; she was only teasing."

Merry's eyes drifted toward the front of the pub where several guests were having drinks—as if to tell her father he had made a public fool of himself. The second part of her wordless retort was less obvious: she extracted gold coins from her pocket and proceeded to count out twenty of them on the table in front of her father. Then she gave one to her mother, for no apparent reason, and three to her brother. "For your education," she said to Orchard.

He picked up the coins, rolled them in his palm, put them down again, picked them up one at a time, and finally said to Merry, "I'll take them." Not even then did his eyes connect with hers.

"You're welcome," she said sarcastically. "I'm tired, and the squirrel is tough. I'm going back to bed."

When she had left the table, no one spoke for a long

time. Orchard watched his father separate the twenty coins into two stacks. "Ten apiece," Rain muttered before he lowered his head into his hands and sobbed.

Only Merry knew that the two old men, the batkeepers he had disposed of the previous day, had been his first murders.

CHAPTER ELEVEN

A Year In The Vortex

The first revolutionary battle had been small, swift and violent—between Colonists and the crew of *Monz*. The second spanned a year and was fought between advocates of truth (the anarchists) and guardians of sanity (World Government). The weaponry were concepts, and the battlefield the public mind. Each volly added spin and breadth to the idelogical vortex tightening over the capital city.

Sometime during the fifteenth month of the year 4110, the anarchists established a sizeable printing facility. Infidel's famous essay on happiness fell like snow upon the city from ingeniously rigged balloons. The so-called Anarchist Press also disseminated interpretations of events about which it claimed to have documented proof, such as this item dated 4d-16m 4110:

> When it was learned that the crew of *Watchful Monz* had engaged Colonists at Syrdo, two freighters were already enroute to the depot planet. *Eldry's Plume* was instructed to return to World, while the more distant *Marsh Fire* was ordered to land on Syrdo and confirm the reports made to Parliament by the *Monz* survivors.
>
> The pilot of *Marsh Fire* yesterday radioed back that he found the Syrdo depot "strewn all over the airless desert." The irate pilot requested permission to proceed to the Nya system and similarly wipe out the Ky base on Ru. Parliament instructed him: "*Marsh Fire* is to take no such action. The Ru facility—as in fact all supposed Ky property—belongs to all people. To destroy it would be to destroy our own holdings. Your crew is, further,

constrained from divulging their observations to the public, at risk of imprisonment."

The Anarchist Press also issued bulletins irregularly, which purported to carry news of life at the Colony, such as the following, dated 12d-17m 4110:

> This month, the Nyasport Town Council agreed to encourage development of a cooperative enterprise which would investigate, for a fee, the quality of currency issued by the separate banks, and which would suggest standards of exchange among the metals and gems used for currency. While no citizen is compelled to employ the service, and no bank need submit to the new agency's scrutiny, and no action can be taken by the agency or the Council even if fraud is uncovered—it is believed that the best banks will, to maintain a reputation for honesty and value, cooperate.

And this report dated 2d-18m 4110:

> The Freeport Home Insurance Company has found itself obliged to establish and maintain a permanent fire department to protect its investments. Forest Singer, grandson of the great Isle Firemaker, has consented to be honorary chief for the fire fighters, who replace the inadequate volunteer brigade established in 4052.

In an editorial, the Ayatsport Press stated: "It's difficult to say which makes the anarchists seem more demented—the idea that the Ky reports are false, or the idea that they are true!"

16d-18m 4110: A bomb exploded in the main office of the Ayatsport Press, and two suspected Ky sympathizers were arrested at the scene. The two pleaded innocence, claiming they had been called by the editor for an interview. But as no one at the Press had any knowledge of any such interview, the two were quickly convicted and executed.

3d-19m 4110: Parliament issued a memo to publishers in Ayatsport and throughout the World. It said simply:

> Henceforth the word *anarchy*, and all its forms, are prohibited. The word will be deleted from the next editions of the Dictionary and the Encyclopaedia. Palace etymologists have determined that the word serves no

unique function, and that the words *crime*, *chaos*, and *purposeless*, and all their forms, amply cover all connotations and contexts where *anarchy* previously was used.

On that same date, a memo went out to all law-enforcement branches. It called for intensifying the search for the "so-called Anarchist Press" and their illegal radio facilities—which evidently were sophisticated enough to eavesdrop on Palace and Spaceport channels. An apparent afterthought offered "luxurious housing and Class One social privileges to the policeman or citizen who supplies information leading to the apprehension of the traitor known as Infidel."

16d-19m 4110: A member of Parliament was assassinated as he crossed near Ayat's Tree on his way from the Palace to his dormitory. A twelve-year-old girl was found there wandering in a daze carrying the murder weapon. She was shot down on the spot. The blame was placed on unspecified criminal elements.

10d-20m 4110: On the first day of the Year's End religious rituals, the Chief Priest of Ayatsport Cathedral, in his address to World keepers of the faith, called for a sense of proportion on the part of citizens of Ayatsport, Stormsville, and all surrounding towns. Here is an excerpt:

> There is no conspiracy; nor is there any great increase of crime in the streets. From time to time there is an unrest born of laziness that comes into public view. We see one now. And laziness is a product of backsliding, of relinquishing our hold on civilization, on Godliness!! Look to the Heavens! The symbols of all goodness and right move toward their great Conclave, the alignment of planets which will occur next year. As you know, such a moment happens but once in a thousand years and constitutes a time of testing for all Mankind—here and at the Colony. Godlessness must be eliminated, else we all share in the wrath of disapproving Gods, all the Gods, who will look upon us and judge us jointly at Conclave!

12d-20m 4110: A dragnet of police regulars, deputized friends of the law, and ordinary citizens swept through Ayatsport—north from the reservoir, south to the

Spaceport—searching every building in their path. More than five-hundred arrests were made. A printing plant in the East Borough and two radio set-ups were found and their equipment confiscated.

Three days later, however, balloons dropped the most voluminous load of papers to date over Ayatsport. One of the papers carried a transcript dating from well after the all-city raid; it was the essence of a conversation between Isle Firemaker and his grandson on Ky. The transcript contained these damaging lines:

> Isle Firemaker: "I understand you have become a leader of men."
> Forest Singer: "I'm among those to whom the free citizens of Ky look for leadership."

The conversation was otherwise innocuous; it was clear that the two men expected their conversation to be monitored.

The underground was never organized. Anyone who so wished could initiate a "discussion group," populate it with those of his choosing, and conduct business in any way he chose. Intercellular contact was infrequent if at all, and in this way the rebels were protected against discovery by chain reaction. As the movement in support of Ky and anarchist ideals grew, so did its reverence for the mysterious Infidel—who seemed able to put their most obscure dreams and ideals into words, words that carried the conviction of righteousness.

And a peculiar practice sprang up, and word of its effect spread through the underground. It became conventional for each cell meeting to have as a silent guest of honor a stranger draped under a black sheet. It came to be firmly believed that on occasion, the real Infidel did visit cell meetings under just such a protective disguise. Perhaps that quiet, almost inanimate black mound there in the dark corner, near the cellar stairs, at the attic ladder, by the boulders beneath the bridge, beneath the tree on a starbrightened country slope... perhaps that was the *real* Infidel!

As we now know, there was no single "Anarchist Press," but its largest facility existed beneath an abandoned warehouse in the Port District, at the intersection of Southwind and Shark. Merry Weaver disclosed its location to Sky Tinsmith—while advising him to go nowhere near it. It was too large, too noisy, and in too obvious a hiding place, she maintained. It may have been her very insistence upon the dangers that prompted Sky to defy caution and make his way stealthily through the dark dock streets, on the evening of 1d-1m 4111, New Year's night, the balmy first night of summer, to the warehouse.

CHAPTER TWELVE

The Warehouse

Sky paused under a shelter of old planks, where an abandoned church was being demolished. This was opposite the Inn of the Frog. He frowned as he read the large sign in the Frog's front window: KY SYMPATHIZERS NOT WELCOME HERE. It made no sense; if Merry's father had placed it there to protect his establishment, he had overlooked the fact that it also served as a beacon proclaiming: there are anarchists in this area. He would have to speak to Merry about it. He moved on.

Half the streetlights were burned out, and there were no suns in the sky. The brightest illumination came from worklights at the atomic plant, several blocks away. He was a fugitive from the police, from citizens who might wonder at his furtive travels, and from robbers prowling the shadows.

At the intersection of Southwind and Flying Fish he pushed himself into a doorway recess—attempting to blend with the dark weather-worn wood. Three police cars passed, their headlights extinguished, and continued slowly on toward the activity at the piers on the River of Reeds. They did not pass the anarchists' warehouse, which was a block out of their path.

At the side door of the warehouse, he unfolded his cloak of secrecy, draped it over his head, and entered without knocking. He had been careful to wear shoes and clothes under it that would not betray his clerical station.

"You are trespassing," said a voice in the gray-black.

"And there is a knife at your back."

"I am Infidel," Tinsmith said.

"On what page of the economics essay appears the line: 'What a man earns through chosen labor is his alone; what he earns through unchosen labor goes into a moral account with which, one day, he will buy his freedom'?"

"Three."

"Remove your disguise and join us, friend. Infidel has already arrived."

"Either there will be two Infidels this night, or I must leave in secret, as I came." He heard the man behind him sheath his knife. The windows were not quite opaque with dirt, and Sky was beginning to see a little through his thin black sheet.

"That would be ludicrous! If we admit two of you, soon everyone will want to cloak themselves in black."

"That might be a good safety measure."

"I can't make the decision alone."

"Can't you—in the spirit of individual responsibility?" Sky could see that his adversary was tall and muscular, dressed as a dock hand. "Is there a way I can observe without the others seeing me?" he asked, his confidential tone inviting the man to use his imagination.

The man said thoughtfully, perhaps daring to hope he addressed the real Infidel. "That's a curious request; it defeats the purpose of your wearing... or does it?" He led the black ghost slowly toward the far end of the empty, musty-smelling warehouse. He lifted a large trap in the floor; the sound of chugging machinery issued from the exposed square hole, and an unsteady light played faintly over descending steps.

A few candles lighted the hallway that led to a large room in which there were about forty people, an operating electric press, and rows of metal shelves that held stacks and stacks of printed papers. Soon after Sky had entered, there was a metallic thunk and then the descending whine of a motor: the press had been turned off. He heard voices behind him and a sound he assumed was that of the trap door being bolted from the inside.

Sky Tinsmith, Infidel, experienced enormous excitement as he entered this most elaborate of all bastions of free thought on World. Though he was their informal leader and their symbol of hope, he felt their inferior. He, after all, spent nearly all his hours in the fortress of sanctuary that was Ayatsport Cathedral; while these people, like Merry Weaver, lived in the real world and daily risked their lives for an idea.

The participants were milling about, talking softly, laughing occasionally, beginning to take their places in a wide circle on the floor. A loud whistle brought Tinsmith's attention to a kettle on a kerosene hot-plate; herb tea was being brewed for all. He spotted his impersonator sitting in one of the few chairs in dim light near a stack of paper rolls. This Infidel wore a black cloak with the familiar signature symbol—the two legs of a triangle, the arrow, the wings—stencilled on his chest. Under the privacy of his plain black sheet, Sky smiled and thought: What a nice idea! The eyes of many of the rebels were looking from Sky to the other symbolic guest.

"I ask the group's indulgence," said the dock worker who had brought Sky down. "I have reason to believe that one of the enshrouded men may be the real Infidel." There were gasps and murmurs. "I think we have no choice but to assume they both are."

Sky chose to sit on the floor on the outskirts of the group. Two assistants distributed papers, the Press' recent publications; and the meeting really began with the entrance into the circle of a tall, heroic-looking young man Sky had heard called River. Presumably this was the leader of this cell, the manager of the Press, and, Sky was led to believe, the inventor of the balloon drops. His face seemed to beam honesty and glow with a melancholy benevolence. With a kindly but hollow feeling, Sky thought briefly: Now *he*'s the sort of fellow Merry needs.

"I have some amazing news," River said. "If you've been keeping your computations up to date, you know that soon World and Ky will be at opposition. Already the light-time between us is over seventy-four minutes—"

"What's the shortest light-time?" a woman, probably a newcomer, asked.

The man sitting beside her whispered hoarsely, "Thirty-two and a half. Ask questions later."

River continued. "We are approaching a communications black-out for the time when there will be two suns between us and Ky; and with the relay on Syrdo inoperative, radio is useless. Yesterday Forest Singer sent us a brief message—which was also heard at the Palace, of course. He plans to send a report addressed to all the World, across the seventy-five-minute gulf, when the planets are once more in line of sight. Everyone here with a radio will be able to hear his message, which will call for peace and understanding and will contain a report on the success of anarchy at Nyasport."

The effect of this announcement was profound. Some applauded, some shouted happily, a few broke into tears.

"But the broadcast will be futile," River continued, "a wasted opportunity, unless we pave the way for it. The Government will surely try to confiscate or render inoperative every licensed radio in the world. Forest will be addressing only the void of space unless we make available vast quantities of illegal receivers." He extracted a small stack of folded papers from his pocket. "We have an elaborate plan."

Sky was sure he ought to have said *I* have a plan; his admiration for this leader was becoming boundless.

"Phase one is to drop from balloons these drawings with which anyone can construct a simple crystal receiver," River continued. "Copies of this are already on their way to Stormsville; from there they will be passed along to other cities downstream on the River of Reeds. Whoever receives them will be instructed to pass them along. In the same drop will be a communique of a new sort: an open letter to our sympathizers. From now on, many of our plans will be shouted to the World—along with our dreams. In this way we can overcome the difficulty we've had due to the movement's lack of organization and contact, one group with the other. And our identities and meeting places can still be kept secret."

A member raised her hand. "But River—a crystal receiver for an interplanetary microwave transmission?"

He shook his head. "Long-wave," he said, and clearly chose to say no more. Somehow the message was to be converted and rebroadcast.

"Quiet!" a man demanded, getting to his feet.

The ceiling above them creaked, and creaked again. Then all was silent.

River said, "Sometimes... when the temperature changes...." But he was still listening. Finally he resumed: "We have an additional plan; call it Phase Two, which will not be announced in an open letter and must be kept secret. I'm going to tell you about it, because I'll need your help with wiring and rigging radio components—"

"Where are you getting the components?" asked a man's voice. It came from the ersatz Infidel off by the paper rolls. His voice stopped the meeting, and all eyes turned to him. By convention, the symbolic Infidel was not supposed to speak.

River shook his head. Such information was not to be divulged. He seemed to study the dark shape for a moment, then proceeded: "The exact nature of Phase Two... will be discussed at our next meeting. I suggest we turn now to the forum. Have we general questions for one another, not relating to the plan?"

"Must we be atheists?" a young man asked. "I have tried to see the planets and suns as meaningless and purposeless, but such a position, well, frightens me; leaves me feeling, well, lonely."

River shrugged. "Many anarchists are religious," he said, apparently excluding himself from their number. "I'm not sure why you ask the question."

"I need to know if you are asking me to give up my Gods along with my Government."

Sky stirred. "May I answer?" he asked gently. "The other Infidel has spoken, so it seems I might as well."

River grinned and shrugged. "Sure, go ahead."

"The boy fails to consider the very principle of freedom. The Colonists are not all atheists, any more than the anarchists of World are. Anarchy holds that anyone may believe and act as his own conscience dictates; anarchy is a political principle, not an ethical one. Infidel himself is a devout man."

"Forest Singer—" River began.

"Is an atheist," Sky admitted.

"You know that Infidel is a devout man?"

"I—it's evident from his essays."

"I have a question," an attractive middle-aged woman said. "Who's throwing all these bombs and committing all these crimes of violence? And why in the World isn't the Government blaming them on us? Can you imagine a better scapegoat for them?"

A man continued the logic: "And are we endangering our own cause by publicizing our opposition to Parliament and the status quo, at the very time when—from some quarter—the status quo is under vicious, violent attack? Aren't we indirectly admitting responsibility for the crimes?"

River nodded. "Good questions. Any answers?" He called on the dock worker who had been watchman at the door.

"They *are* blaming us in a way," he said. "We're being set up. The Ayatsport Press keeps referring to a vague criminal element—meaning us. When the time comes, they'll have a list of our supposed crimes longer than your arm. Then they'll say the criminal element has been identified as a band calling themselves anarchists. Only there isn't any such word any more."

"You can't think," said a woman incredulously, "that Parliament is committing murders just to have something to blame on us!"

"I don't know," the dock worker said.

"They're reluctant," said River, "to admit that World is at odds with Ky—I think—because they don't want people here getting ideas—like wanting political freedom. I think they figure they'll just ignore us, and Ky, until the whole unpleasantness loses steam and just goes away. That's why we have to keep telling what we know, making sure we build more and more steam—"

"And telling the truth," said Sky, "just because it *is* the truth."

River smiled at him.

At that instant there was a chilling noise. To some it sounded like a woman's scream; to others it was the screech made when metal spikes are being torn out of wood.

The false Infidel leapt to his feet.

River, deftly as a magician, pulled a pistol from his trousers and fired it. The projectile hit the Infidel and tore him apart before he could even shout with surprise.

Sky sat spellbound, confused. Then he and the others heard the clatter of footfalls coming from the corridor.

River yanked the sheet off the false Infidel to reveal the bloody remains of a man wearing the forest-green shirt of the Palace Police; his severed hand clutched a small transmitter. As the group members scrambled to their feet, their eyes wide with fear, River grabbed Sky Tinsmith and hurried him to the backside of the press.

"Trust me, dear friend," River insisted as he removed Sky's cloak and in the same movement draped it over himself. He pushed Sky into the heart of the press, between the rollers and the lower plate, then clipped a metal cover over the side to hide the valuable outlaw.

Sky only heard the rest. The door was broken open. There were screams and shots and the sounds of struggle.

"Look who we have here!" a policeman said. Presumably he had removed the black cloak from River.

"You have only another one of the millions of us," River said.

"I think we caught ourselves the Infidel!" said another policeman.

In an appallingly few minutes, Sky was left alone in disheartening silence. He found that he was holding a clump of papers. Near the top of one was the heading: PHASE TWO. Though he was still shaking from shock and fear, Sky had the presence of mind to think: I'll have to get Merry to take this to Stormsville.

That same night, Merry Weaver was at the Palace of Parliament attending a state dinner to honor the new members of Parliament. She was escorted by a past-Parliamentarian, a rather famous lawyer who sometimes served on panels of judges. He was middle-aged, immaculately and expensively dressed, on the stout side, a man who was popular for the brightness of his frequent smiles.

CHAPTER THIRTEEN

The Flying Pig

An authority cannot claim credit for apprehending villains whose existence remains in doubt. Following the warehouse raid, bits of information seeped out through the Ayatsport Press, as in the following item:

> Recent discoveries lead to the conclusion that a real conspiracy may exist here and at Ky Colony, an ideological movement bent on the annihilation of civilization as we know it. Last evening, a roundup of these criminals was undertaken successfully by Palace and Ayatsport Police, who jointly raided a warehouse at Southwind and Shark, in the Port District. This was known to be their headquarters. A printing press and radio facilities were found, and twenty-nine men and women taken prisoner.

And this a few days later:

> Palace sources reveal that the leader of the Ky rebels is the self-styled outlaw philosopher known to some as "Infidel"—who may be responsible for the attempt made on Isle Firemaker's life, 5d-7m 4110, during the *Watchful Monz* parade.

And this follow-up:

> It is believed that one of the chaotics arrested in the Port District raid is the infamous Infidel. A man calling himself only "River" is now being interrogated. The other twenty-eight captured in that raid have been sentenced to die ignobly, all in the same grave.

Many people joked about the Colony's "tantrums and

fits," and ridiculed the foisting of chaos as a new kind of order.

At club meetings, entertainers prompted gales of laughter with their readings of parodies of Infidel's essays, "plucked damp from the gutter," as one comic put it; and an old popular song was resurrected. Though it was a shade off-color, the Press reproduced the catchy ditty, subtitling it A CHAOTIC'S LAMENT:

"The Flying Pig"

Mother Pig pranced around
On her six stubby legs,
While her brood waddled hungrily behind.
Mother's teats dragged the ground,
And her brood slurped the dregs,
But a piglet was of contrary mind:

He didn't want to drink;
He didn't want to care;
He didn't want to think;
He didn't want to share;
He didn't want to work;
He didn't want to try;
That bumpkin wanted—
That hayseed wanted—
That fool pig wanted to fly!

Mother Pig shed a tear
When her boy flapped his feet,
And her brood laughed hysterically and looked.
He put jets in his rear;
'Twas too late for retreat.
Wha-wha-whoosh! His little ham was cooked.

(Repeat chorus)

That peabrain wanted—
That screwball wanted—
That dead pig wanted to fly!

The Flying Pig

jaunty

MOTHER PIG PRANCED AROUND ON HER SIX STUBBY LEGS WHILE HER BROOD WADDLED
MOTHER PIG SHED A TEAR WHEN HER BOY FLAPPED HIS FEET AND HER BROOD LAUGHED HYS-

HUNGRILY BEHIND. MOTHER'S TEATS DRAGGED THE GROUND AND HER BROOD SLURPED THE
-TERICALLY AND LOOKED. HE PUT JETS IN HIS REAR, 'TWAS TOO LATE FOR RE-

DREGS. BUT A PIGLET WAS OF CONTRARY MIND.
-TREAT. WHA-WHA-WHOOOSH! HIS LITTLE HAM WAS COOKED.

CHORUS
SECOND VERSE
CHORUS
FINAL ENDING

HE DIDN'T WANT TO DRINK · HE DIDN'T WANT TO CARE · HE DIDN'T WANT TO THINK · HE

DIDN'T WANT TO SHARE · HE DIDN'T WANT TO WORK · HE DIDN'T WANT TO TRY · THAT

BUMPKIN WANTED · THAT HAYSEED WANTED · THAT FOOL PIG WANTED TO FLY! · THAT

slowly
PEABRAIN WANTED · THAT SCREWBALL WANTED · THAT DEAD PIG WANTED TO FLY!

Woodcutter, O
9d 6m 3995
Ayalsport
NP 239170

CHAPTER FOURTEEN

A Gull Envious Of The Bears

Passing Sky Tinsmith in the Cathedral Rotunda, one experienced priest said to another, "His sudden happiness is a sad thing to behold." The other answered, "The boy is troubled—in his soul."

They were right.

Following his near capture at the warehouse, Sky had fled, terrified, to the safety of the Cathedral. He quickly re-established old friendships and began to socialize more with other seminarians. They found him surprisingly bright. "Tinsmith has finally come out of it!" a young priest declared. "Yes," said another, "but what was it he was *in*?"

Sky Tinsmith was forced to show his good cheer, in order to hide the fact that he feared—not for his life, but for its value. His trip to the warehouse had been an attempt to prove to himself that he possessed physical courage. It seemed to prove the opposite. He knew he could never have acted, in the face of death, as River had acted in saving him. Sky Tinsmith was a brain envious of the muscles of the body, a gull envious of the bears. The finger of blame in his mind stoppered his flow of thought; he stopped writing.

His facade of gregariousness was doubly dishonest; for he cultivated it to serve him as an alibi. Petty liars, he reasoned are not fit to be leaders of men. Who am I to advise others to take risks?

He was in this state of mind when word came down to him from the Chief Priest that he, Sky Tinsmith, had been called to testify at the session of Parliament commencing on 10d-8m 4111.

His colleagues at the Cathedral toasted him with wine. "What a great honor!" they exclaimed.

An odd thing followed this announcement: Sky became his old reclusive, soft-spoken, serious self again. His fear had not left him, nor had his self-estimate risen. It was merely that he thought: Good, it is over; I have been caught.

The night before he was to report to the Palace, Sky slipped down to his sanctum—for the last time, he assumed (and he was right, but not for the reasons he feared)—to write his last paper.

It was an apology on a single page—not recanting his positions, but confessing his lack of bravery and blaming that for the movement's failings. It also served as a will bequeathing his only possessions of value, his essays, to "the Children of Ky." He ended the page with the two marks of Infidel's symbol, not so flamboyantly etched as before, then printed five hundred copies and left them on the sewer landing for Merry to find.

CHAPTER FIFTEEN

The Hero And The Anarchist

Sky Tinsmith arrived early for what he felt was sure to be his execution. He entered the Garden of Gods through the normally public gate, and found it swarming with Palace Police—two of whom accosted him, demanded to see his identity papers, and held his arms while his name was being checked on a master list carried by their sergeant.

"Dormitory A," the sergeant instructed.

Whereupon the two guards instantly released Sky's arms. The action carried the connotation of new-found respect.

"Follow us, please," one of the guards requested of Sky; his tone further implied: We regret the inconvenience, but surely you understand our need for caution.

Sky was puzzled, but no less frightened.

Dormitory A, within the Garden itself, is a five-story rock horseshoe hidden by a small forest of ironwoods; it shelters an exquisite labyrinthine garden—a zoo carved of hedges, a spectrum of flowers—through which one passes to reach an elevator within a square column of iron lace. Gardeners work perpetually, now as on that day four years ago, at their living work of art.

While on the path to the elevator, Sky had the thought: If it weren't for all the guards about, what a spot this would be for an ambush! In the center of the garden, near where workmen were installing a fountain of rising stone lilies, stood a man—whom Sky, in his daze of apprehension, did not at once recognize.

"This Witness is my guest," the man said, showing a paper to prove his contention.

Sky's escorts glanced perfunctorily at the permit, nodded, and turned to leave.

Relief and curiosity cleared the young seminarian's mind, and his knees buckled as he first looked into the face of his benefactor. "Firemaker!" he gasped, tears welling in his eyes.

"Good to see you, my friend," the hero said dryly, warning Sky to collect himself.

When the guards were out of sight, Firemaker briefly took the frightened young man into his arms—the tall hero and the small anarchist looking like the father and son they felt themselves to be in that instant.

Firemaker sat with Sky at a garden bench, took his hand firmly and said, "Listen to what I'm *nòt* going to say, Sky Tinsmith. I am as trusted as any man alive. In my quarters we can speak confidentially, without worrying about listening devices; but I advise against it. If you should need my help, I can give it only out of ignorance. I have lived my life as I've wished to. I have no political ideas."

"Surely you—"

"No, I haven't. Do you know why you have been called as a Witness?"

"I assume it—"

"If you must assume, don't do it out loud. You have been called as an expert on the religious implications of Conclave—the alignment of planets."

"But—you mean that's all? Why wouldn't they choose a famous theologian?"

"Theologians have been called, too. You were selected at the Cathedral because you are thought to represent a more liberal, more scientific, more youthful point of view."

"I'm afraid I talk too much."

"I wouldn't be surprised. You're talking too much now. Whenever a stranger comes to Parliament, I have the same advice for him; and I'll give it to you: Choose your words with deadly care."

"Are you warning me that—?"

"I can assist you in matters of protocol."

"Uh, what's the hatchling?"

"A lizard, I think."

"Isn't it a pleasant day?"

Firemaker laughed. "It really is good to see you again, Sky. I've missed you these last few years; I'm looking forward to the time we'll have together."

"And you can't know how... relieved I am to see you again. Here's an ordinary enough question for you: Why are there so many Palace Police all over the Garden? I'm sure that's not normal—even when Parliament is in session."

Firemaker searched his pockets and found a folded scrap of paper. "These were found strewn throughout the Garden about six days ago."

Sky unfolded and read it; it said: "Forest Singer will speak to the people of the World 13d-8m 4111, and his words will strike down Parliament like lightning. And the World will be free."

Sky said, "Just an overly dramatic boast."

Firemaker shook his head. "The Government is taking it as a bomb threat."

CHAPTER SIXTEEN

The Reluctant Hatchling

At noon an east wind blew waves of sound, from trumpeters in the tree-trunk turrets of the Palace, across the Garden of Gods and into the nearest streets of Ayatsport. The herald meant that the hatchling had been nested; Parliament was being called to the Glen; the session that eventually was to be called the Congress of Ky was about to commence.

(The session ought to have been called, according to tradition, the Congress of the Lizard—as previous sessions were dubbed the Congress of the White Bat, the Congress of the Spine Fish, the Congress of the Marsh Fly, and so on, back far beyond Unity to the reign of Kinbi; for on 10d-8m 4111 a lizard egg had been brought from the remote province of Red Sands to call Parliament to order.)

"Ah! If it isn't my gouty opponent from Artesia. How have you been since last session?"

"Just as I was before last session. What do you think—will this dreadful Colony thing dominate the session?"

"No doubt. We won't get to domestic matters for a month at least!"

These two worthy gentlemen were ambling along the colonnade outside the Glen. One was dressed as a crane, the other as a hippopotamus.

Someone came in whistling the jaunty strains of "The Flying Pig," and this caused a sprinkle of laughter, during which a few others joined in and sang the concluding lines in three-note harmony.

Isle Firemaker, Sky Tinsmith, and Sagacious Harvester relaxed leaning against the cold marble of the petrified palms in the colonnade. They watched the gathering Parliamentarians and dignitaries and engaged in small talk.

"Isn't that old Thorn Trapper headed this way?" Harvester asked.

Firemaker shook his head. "Trapper died four years ago, while you were at Ky. That's the representative from the South Island States—Miller, I think his name is."

"I hear the States want a causeway linking them to the mainland," Harvester said.

Sky Tinsmith thought of a ball in space chained to a larger sphere which spun it endlessly around. He thought that all these men and women impersonating, deifying, mindless animals were the only ones capable of severing the chain.

At four hours past noon, a rumor spread that physicians had heard scratching within the lizard shell, but that the little spheroid was still intact.

Near sunset, carts were wheeled in containing fruit and wine. Some took their supper on into the Glen; others clustered in picnics among the colonnade palms.

A young woman, a newly elected Member of Parliament, happened to join Firemaker's group outside. A pretty face was partially hidden beneath the headpiece that completed her transformation into a toad; and her talkativeness was unexpectedly pleasant.

"Oh, they haven't caught the real Infidel," she declared. "My father knows the Prefect of South Borough police, who told him this River fellow was probably just a leg man. I don't think they'll ever catch the real one."

"Why not?" Sky asked, biting into a nut-apple.

"Because now that his ideas are well known, anyone can become Infidel. Catch one, and another one will come to life. Spontaneous regeneration." She laughed. "*I* even wrote an Infidel essay once. Awful, rambling lot of sentiment; but it was—" She cut herself off, as if suddenly afraid she might be misunderstood.

"It was heartfelt?" Sky asked.

"I'm not an anarchist!" she exclaimed.

"Of course not," Firemaker said, to calm her.

80

"Although," she continued, eating while she talked, "if it weren't for the fact that the bastards kill people, I'd say their extreme position might be a healthy thing. Jolt some of these guys—" she waved with her wine glass toward the entrance to the Glen "—jolt them out of their complacency. Get rid of some of the molasses of traditionalism. Can you believe the most important men in the World are sitting around here killing time waiting for a lizard to hatch?" She nudged her toad head. "And you can't tell me that Parliament on Ky still wears these cute little animal suits."

"There is no Parliament on Ky," Sky said, amused.

That shocked her into thoughtful silence. "How do you know? That's the official line of the anarchists, but surely it's an exaggeration. They must have some sort of—"

"Only informal meetings," Harvester said.

"How do you know?" she persisted.

"I am, I was, Ambassador Harvester," he introduced himself belatedly.

"I wondered," she said as her eyes darted involuntarily to where his right arm should have been. "Is the Colony a beautiful place? What do people act like there when there's no police? Aren't they terribly suspicious of everybody. Do those who can't buy food and clothing run around naked and starving? Are they really all atheists?"

Harvester laughed. "The answer to most of that is a qualified no. Wouldn't you say, gentlemen?"

"It's a beautiful place, if you like deserts," Sky said. "And there's at least one large church in Nyasport."

"I'm sure," said Firemaker, "that they rely rather heavily on private security services. They did even before they—"

"All *three* of you have been to Ky? Gods alive! Are you... you're Isle Firemaker! Oh, I feel like such an idiot! Gods alive, here I've been chattering away, acting like such an idiot! Idiot! You must think—"

Sky managed to get her out of her corner by asking, "Are you finding wide-spread support for anarchist ideas in—where did you say you were from?"

"Stormsville. No, *nothing* intellectual is widespread in Stormsville. But I've met some pretty intelligent people who don't, well, who don't dismiss Infidel out of hand. He's got them curious."

Sky said, smiling rather abstractly, "He's got you interested, anyway. That's interesting."

"Oh *please* don't label me a supporter of anarchy, or chaos, or whatever we're supposed to be calling it these days. Everybody knows all this freedom talk is just a complicated way of saying it would be fun to be a little more irresponsible than we're currently allowed to be."

An hour or so later, President Lightman walked by, took Firemaker aside and said to him, "In case we have been thinking along different lines, old friend, I feel I should warn you that the Central Committee has decided that this Ky insurrection is the only possible source of war for a World united under one Government. Eventually, if not from the outset, that philosophy will surely underlie this session of Parliament. You mustn't challenge it. Not even you could emerge unscathed from any expression of sympathy for the Colony—or for your grandson."

"I won't challenge you personally," Firemaker said. "I don't advocate war, crime, murder or chaos; and I won't back their practitioners. But I will present whatever argument might seem necessary to be sure that not too much philosophy remains 'underlying.' I don't favor ignorance or subterfuge any more than I favor crime."

A page at the Gateway to the Glen clanged a bell and cried succinctly, "The hatching, the hatching...."

President Lightman peered into Firemaker's eyes and frowned. He seemed dissatisfied with what he saw there.

CHAPTER SEVENTEEN

The Glen

Most citizens have seen drawings or paintings of the Glen—in particular Brick Marksman's famous color rendering which appears in so many texts—but no representation conveys the overwhelming effect of Parliament's meeting place. In it, time seems solid, history a visible thing.

The rule of King Toitu ended in a conflagration which gutted a large central portion of the Palace; and it was there, nearly a century later, that the Glen was built. King Bastonetu, who is credited with having invented representative government, personally supervised its construction.

Structurally, the great chamber is in the shape of an egg—seventy-two meters long (one meter for each of the chapters in The Book of Syrdo). Built before the availability of aluminum, structural steel modules, reinforced concrete, or any of the common machines in use today, the titanic egg was fabricated by boatbuilders from wood beams and slats, and buttressed with hand-carved shapes of granite. Iron straps, spikes and a resin made from palm sap hold the pieces in place.

It is said that once the interior had been coated with plaster, and before the decorative fixtures were added, the perfection of the shape gave workmen vertigo. They found themselves in a formless, featureless environment in which sound came not from its source, and light and shadow only added to the visual confusion.

The only features interrupting the perfection of the chamber—which had no floor, ceiling or walls—were the oaken doors, the Gateway, at the small end of the egg, and the circular hole over the large end, which would seat the great dome.

Four glassmen—one of whom was Friend Inventor—spent nine years constructing the dome. It measures twenty meters in diameter at the base (for the twenty months) and is sixteen meters high (for the sixteen days of the months). While there are several iron bars within it for main support, the shape is largely held together by its own design and weight. The scene of the dome, made of bits of stained glass held fast by lead wire, is the picture one might find looking straight up in a forest of gigantic trees.

While the dome was being installed, artisans from all over the World decorated the interior. Sheet iron, invited to rust decoratively, was pounded into the shapes of tree trunks and limbs, while gold, silver, and brass were poured into leaf molds. Painters frescoed the walls as an evening sky over a deep green slope. Sculptors carved mammoth slabs of sequoia into mushroom-shaped desks and chairs like tangles of vines. Decorators brought in flowers made of gems and planted them among the rusting tree trunks and boulders of rounded quartz crystal. Illumination specialists turned candles into fireflies, copper-treated oils into the eerie green of marshglow, alcohol lamps into the blue of Nyaslight, and amber desk lamps into the warmth of Ayat.

The first Parliament ministered to only the Continent of Winds, ruled by democratic King Bastonetu. In 3732, one of the early Parliamentarians, Thistle Bronzeman, wrote: "It is impossible to enter the Glen without being mindful of a peculiar greatness Man can achieve in his ability to humiliate himself before the Gods. In the Glen, we feel diminished—unworthy to administer laws to such men as could build our Glen. We are ever in a prayerful mood, ever looking upward to glimpse Ayat and Nya as they pass over the exquisite dome."

Through succeeding generations, the Glen grew as if it were watered and fertilized. Each year more bejeweled flowers arrived. In the year when aluminum was first reduced for manufacture, a gift of aluminum vines was added to many of the prominent trees. At Unification, part of each nation's tribute to the new World Government were treasures to be added to the Glen. Thus arrived the alabaster menagerie from the Continent of Ice, the gently trickling fountains from Meadowland, the steel-and-platinum ironwoods from the States of the Nation of Monz, the head-high jade ferns from the South Island States, Ayatsport's own gift of electric lights to replace the oil lamps on Members' desks, and countless other treasures of art and craftsmanship. In 4039, the Glen was fully electrified; ventilation ducts were added unobtrusively, and near the top of the dome a mercury-vapor lamp was installed which produced a blinding blue pinpoint to simulate perpetual watchfulness by Nya, Goddess of Truth.

The Glen, all would agree, represents in full the Paradise the Gods expect Man to create upon the face of the World.

CHAPTER EIGHTEEN

The Congress
Of Ky—First Session

"The hatching, the hatching...." called the page; and the picnicking and gossiping men and woman—costumed and in street clothes—ambled toward their stations of duty in the Glen.

Sky Tinsmith approached the Gateway and saw only darkness beyond it; then a few bluish glints of metal caught his eye. Crossing the threshold he faced shining ironwoods; and as his eyes became accustomed to the gloom, he saw beyond them to dark treetrunks. He heard the whispering of fountains mingling with the whispers of people, and saw "fireflies" twinkling over a berry bush fat with rubies. A symphony of emotions played in his soul, and he had no choice but to allow its crescendos.

There—a proud and attentive alabaster fawn; beside it a resting tiger-lizard. Amber lights mixed with blues and greens as he approached the clearing. Without realizing it, he clutched Firemaker's wrist.

As though he were breaking out of a black thicket into a moonlit glade, the universe opened up. Sky found himself at the summit of descending tiers of desks, semi-circled to face the President's Knoll at the deep end of the down-raked Glen. Artificial Nyaslight streamed from above and made the clearing, painted with shadows, seem even more vast than it was.

"There is a single crack in the egg," the Clerk of the Glen said into a microphone.

Firemaker must have led Sky to an assigned desk; for when Sky cleared marvel from his mind he was seated alone. He looked in vain to discover where Firemaker and

Harvester had seated themselves. Faces were hard to see; desk lamps lighted only papers and hands. Sky was, for his day, a free thinker; nevertheless it pleased him to see among the hands many which passed the waiting time by potting tiny sprouts and sending prayers aloft. He felt this was a sign of innate goodness; it gave him hope that justice might be sought in this awesome chamber.

But he was beginning to think like Infidel again. He found the Glen more inspiring than even the Cathedral, but he saw it also as a sign of decadence, a misplacing of priorities, an evidence of the deprivation of the peoples of the World, an insane indulgence in orthodoxy.

A microphone concealed within the nest of silver strands picked up a popping sound; spotlights hidden in the trees picked out the nest on its pedestal on the Knoll; on a signal all in the Glen rose to their feet. The popping increased, then stopped. There was a faint movement at the edge of the nest. Something the size and color of a finger pushed into view. The creature was trying to escape from its overheated abode. It teetered on the top edge then fell to the pedestal where it lay still. (If it had died there, this would have been inconsequential; only an egg that fails to hatch causes legal and superstitious difficulties.)

"The first session of Parliament in this Year of Conclave is called to attention," said the Clerk of the Glen; and all took their seats. "The Gods see Stone Lightman, President of the World, in his thirteenth year of administration before the Glen," continued the Clerk; "the Gods see a humble man of vision, compassion, and a wisdom exceeded only by their own."

The President leaned forward toward his desk microphone as faint spotlights brightened, making him a shade more luminous than any around him. He pronounced the Glen's ritual greeting that has opened every session of Parliament in recorded history, paused, then said, "From your jovial attitudes, ladies and gentlemen of Parliament, I assume you are not in tune with the gravity of this session. Perhaps our intragovernmental information agencies have been lax in their duty to keep you informed. Be that as it may, by the end of this term, we shall have found a way to discredit an idea—or a way to destroy a planet."

There was not a sound to be heard in the Glen; the absence of insect noises seemed supernatural.

He continued: "You will come to agree with me that it is fortuitous that we can begin by hearing testimony from Witnesses of Faith; for our beliefs, too, are under deliberate organized attack. The planets of our system will align themselves twenty-two months from now, and rituals of supplication are underway at the Cathedral. Such a period of testing could not be worse timed, politically; for it falls when animosities against us continue to grow—animosities stemming from Ky and symbolized by the criminal Infidel.

"Hatred for us will doubtless get a boost three days from now, when Forest Singer, known to be the leader of the Colonial atheists—" he was interrupted by a great gasp as those in the Glen recognized the name of their hero's grandson "—will attempt to reach World citizens in an unauthorized broadcast, which many strategists believe will contain a declaration of war." The Glen was silent again; the President added sadly, parenthetically, "Isle Firemaker deserves our boundless sympathy and understanding," then went on in his official voice: "And further complicating matters, Palace Police have reason to suspect that there will be an attempt to detonate a bomb here at the Palace, perhaps in the Glen, at the conclusion of the broadcast from Ky. Be assured there will be no explosion, because the Glen will be searched by security patrols between meetings.

"The atmosphere of Conclave must necessarily influence our deliberations. For this reason, the Central Committee has called three eminent Witnesses on the subject: Stream Mortarman, the most reverend of living theologians; Cliff Sailor, professor of astrophysics from Nyaslight Observatory, who will give us a purely scientific look at Conclave; and Sky Tinsmith, a liberal of the new generation of instructors in the ways of Faith, who is said to be able to synthesize the two views which will precede his. We will hear these Witnesses first, so that we need keep them from their holy work no longer than necessary."

And so, Sky thought, we can be excluded from any talk of war.

The theologian evoked a sweeping sense of communal guilt. Even nonbelievers in the Glen felt at least sneaky by the time the palsied old priest reached his concluding phrase: "As no man breathes air solely his own, as he accomplishes no deed by his hands alone, his crime is your crime. His wretchedness if your wretchedness. His fear of retribution is your fear of retribution. When the Gods meet in Conclave, they will see us as with a single eye and pass sentence not merely upon the unjust but upon the World. We have precious little time to prepare. This criminal element called the Ky people must be subdued—else they destroy us all!"

The scientist tried to restore hope and reason to the Glen, and to some extent succeeded. Following his tedious recitation of planetary distances, measurements of mass, and calculations, concerning their combined gravitational power, he said, "Men of science, even those who pray to the Gods, tend to discount the myth of Conclave. It does seem likely that coincident with one alignment of planets, there was unusual seismic activity here, and it may well have triggered a glacial movement that led to the extinction of numerous species; there have been many alignments since then, however, and apparently no catastrophy resulted—if you look for unbiased evidence outside the religious texts. The gravitational attractions of the bodies in question are simply too faint. The first alignment in civilized times marked the start of our calendar. While religious writings claim there was great devastation Worldwide, archeologists and historians can find no support for the claim. The next alignment occurred in 1422, and of this event we have rather good information. We know that the various peoples of the World hunted down and brutally murdered anyone suspected of the mildest of crimes, that many died of fasting, and that on the night of Conclave there were street riots among those factions not locked behind their doors and terrified—not of their Gods, but of their 'virtuous' neighbors. And nothing happened. Apparently not even the tides were affected by the alignment of planets. Unless we are to assume that the bloody activities of a panicked population averted the wrath of the Gods, we must conclude that the only real source of catastrophy was superstitious fear. I represent a group of scientists and astronomers who believe Conclave presents no physical threat. But we agree wholeheartedly with the Central Committee, and the Cathedral, in their contention that the Ky rebels must be contained at all costs—lest popular fears again unleash an orgy of suspicion and irrational accusation. I concur with the reverend Mortarman in his statement that, 'Whatever calamity befalls us we will bring down upon our own heads,' though in a different way from what he had in mind."

The scientist nodded, indicating his statement was concluded. As he stepped down from the seashell that served as a Witness chair, he received precisely the magnitude of applause that had been granted the theologian; but mixed in it was a smattering of laughter: the little lizard jolted to life, as if a spring had sprung within it, and its tiny legs catapulted it to the scientist's shoulder. The man was amused; he picked it off and laid it gently on the shell-chair, the curve of which acted as an acceleration ramp once the creature's legs were again in motion. It scrambled up the shell and launched itself toward a rusted-iron tree trunk, where its claws made a high screeching sound as it climbed—finally to vanish among the bogus treetops.

"The hour is late," President Lightman said, stopping the laughter. "We shall wait until tomorrow to hear our final Witness on Conclave. We convene at the second hour of dawn and thus establish a regular schedule for the remainder of the session." He sought no sign of approval from either the Parliament or the Central Committee—in defiance of custom. It seemed he wished to railroad the meeting to a close, for some reason of his own. "Will the trumpets please herald close of the Glen?"

CHAPTER NINETEEN

Sleep In A Sanctuary

"You're worried," Sky said to Firemaker. They were still in the dormitory hall, not yet sheltered in the hero's suite. "But you needn't be; I'm all right now—almost looking forward to tomorrow."

"Glad to hear it," Firemaker said as he opened his door.

Dormitory A was an old building with large rooms; Firemaker had three: an office, a library, and a bedroom. They were the man: tall and stately, furnished with the findings of a long life. Machinery dominated the office—a typer, a wire-spool music player, a computer, an astrogation-plate projector, new globes of World and Ky, a desk and chair of cast aluminum. In the library, the largest space, swords and firearms carried the lines of a bold fireplace to the ceiling; a crammed trophy case—looking as old as its dustiest statuette—supported a high case of books; but it was a cool tapestry—a landscape stitched in blues, greens, and sand—that owned the library, as it was the bed—ancient, hand-carved, with a canopy of bronze cloth—that owned the bedroom. Sky felt as comfortable in these rooms as in the presence of their habitant. And as safe.

Sky stopped before the tapestry; he knew the scene: the Valley of Icy Waters—on Ky. "Who did this?" he asked.

"My daughter," Firemaker said. "A good many years ago."

"It's wonderful!"

"She had an exceptional visual talent. May I offer you some wine?"

"I—if it's no trouble."

Firemaker pressed a button by the door. "No trouble at all, not in Dormitory A. Have you looked through the books? There are some from Ky that will interest you...."

Sky had not slept the night before, out of worry; now he was wide awake, out of an unaccustomed feeling of warmth combined with excitement. He was sitting on the floor comparing illustrations in Ky history texts when there was a soft knock at the door.

Firemaker admitted the room clerk with a table of wine and cheeses. There was a large, clear, acorn-shaped bottle on the table, too.

"This," indicated the room clerk, "was delivered for you this morning. Here is the note."

As the clerk backed out of the door, Firemaker glanced at the note and smiled. He said to Sky, "Now we have a choice of wine or something a little stronger. This is from an acquaintance of mine, Friend Warrior."

"The pilot? I've heard of him. Firemaker... you have the strangest look on your face. Is there something you're not telling me?"

Firemaker laughed. "I really don't know. I've been around politicians too long, I guess. I'm beginning to see conspiracies in trivialities. This gift bottle is a generous reminder of a commitment I've made for tomorrow—something that will take me away from the Glen. Since tonight's session ended so abruptly, postponing your testimony until the morning—I'll probably miss your appearance."

"I'll record it for you. Or deliver my speech to you here and now. It won't be long, and I'm not even going to bother with notes—"

"You need sleep tonight. Record it for me; I'd like to hear your applause, too. I'm tempted to cancel my appointment and come to the Glen anyway."

"You know I'd like you to be there, but please don't—"

"It's a dis-winging. Warrior's child is five. Now *that* can't be part of a conspiracy."

"A religious or secular ceremony?"

"A little of both, I gather. There will be good-luck pottings, and they'll read the appropriate passages from

Syrdo; but a surgeon will remove the wings, and the boy will be under anesthetic."

"Good. That's exactly the way that ceremony should be handled. I've always dreaded the possibility that I will be asked someday to perform the orthodox dis-winging. I'm afraid I couldn't."

Firemaker smiled as he poured them strong drinks. "I imagine you could, if you had to."

They listened to quiet music and discussed unimportant matters that seemed terribly important.

Another clerk arrived with a mattress with which he made a bed for Sky on the library floor.

The night was almost black—slightly reddened by dim and distant Monz. Near dawn the red sun flared white for a duration of several seconds, and brightness penetrated the heavy-glass panes in the leaded window by the tapestry. A pattern of distorted squares fell across Sky's undisturbed body. For the first time since the night of the warehouse raid, he did not dream.

CHAPTER TWENTY

The Congress Of Ky—Second Session

The President's opening words convinced Sky he had arrived in an overconfident mood.

"This young priest," he said, "is here before us not so much because he is a leader of men, but because of essays he has written...."

Sky missed the next few words; when his mental smoke cleared, he heard:

"...essays have brought him recognition amongst his elders and contemporaries, who consider Sky Tinsmith in touch with the religious temper of the times. I have read the essays sent me by the Cathedral, and have been quite impressed. The elders say this young man will either help to ease the church into a new era of scientific thought—or perhaps destroy the church altogether."

Sky was dizzy with relief and emboldened by the goodhearted laughter which greeted the President's introduction. He stepped to the shell-chair, almost cocky in his movements; he looked very small against the sweeping mother-of-pearl shape. "President Lightman, Members of Parliament, guests of the State, I am honored to be here," said Sky Tinsmith, said Infidel, addressing the Government of the World. "How may I serve you?"

"Give us your thoughts," said the President, "on Conclave, as it relates to your own religious interpretations, and tell us what we may expect in the way of reactions to the event from the young men and women of your generation."

"I—I don't mean to contradict you, President Lightman, but I don't quite agree with your estimate of the extent to which my ideas are shared. The observations I can offer are based only on my meditation and study. I seldom get out into the World to discuss religion with my peers."

The President nodded. "We accept your disclaimer of omniscience, young man. Just give us your own thoughts."

The little philosopher addressed the tiers of faceless rulers—only their amber hands visible under desk lights—tiers that emanated from the Witness chair like the concentric circles spreading from a pebble dropped in a pond. "I hope," he said, "that at last the age of Nya is upon us, the age of Truth. I believe in the Gods, but I hold them to be great abstractions, spirits, influences. Not mechanical fists over the minds of men. The Gods pull us toward virtue; they do not guarantee justice, or impose literal punishments, or command us to accept whole-cloth the myths of the books of antiquity. What sense does it make for us to persist in the belief that one day, when we have made of our World a paradise, the suns and planets Friend Inventor saw through his telescope will arrive here to consummate a human-type love? The meaning of those myths and admonitions is clear: that we must treat our planet with respect and revere its resources. The Gods have no locales in space; they are omnipresent spirits. The planets and suns are only planets and suns. You wish to know what will happen when the planets stretch out between Ayat and Nya? Ask an astronomer or a geophysicist. You heard an eminent one last night. I take his estimate of the situation to be an accurate one; *he* is the expert.

"The great theologian, Stream Mortarman, must not be ignored, however. He is the cornerstone of the old school, a man proud of his ability to hold his Faith in contradiction to the scientific observations of a thousand years; and he represents the thinking of millions. I believe Parliament ought to take a stance openly in favor of the scientific interpretation of Conclave, openly discouraging the orthodox interpretation that is far more likely to promote panic than sudden virtue."

When he had finished, there was an odd moment of

silence, out of which someone in the far reaches of the Glen said, "Hear hear!" Then there was an applause the shape of which was seldom heard in Parliament. It began timidly, as great numbers clapped their palms lightly, then, when it became clear everyone was doing it, the ovation became a roar of approval.

"I'm surprised they haven't kicked you out of the Cathedral," the President said lightly. "But I confess I personally respond to your line of reasoning. I thought you might feel a little freer to speak your mind if we didn't put you on immediately following your elder. Was I right?"

Sky grinned. "Oh, I don't know. The Cathedral heirarchy are familiar with my... my notions."

"How about your political notions?"

"Sir?"

"Concerning, for example, organization versus chaos?"

"I don't know what you're asking me."

"I think you do."

"Are you asking what I think of the Ky rebellion?"

"Indirectly. You needn't speak in particulars."

Sky suddenly felt hot, as if the mother-of-pearl cradling him had become infra-red.

"Come now, Tinsmith, you'll not convince us that you have no opinion."

"I—I don't think the violence perpetrated in their name is consistent with their ideas."

"Then you are on intimate terms with their ideas?"

Sky was a bad pretender. His compulsive honesty was urging him to use this once-in-a-lifetime platform to plead his case—even though his execution would immediately follow. His intellect told him he could serve better, and longer, if he skirted the truth. He noticed that his volume had dropped and his hands were sweating; he resolved to hear his intellect, to brighten his demeanor and take the matter as lightly as possible. He resolved to try, but there was a fear—like the carrier wave of a broadcast beam—telling him he could deceive no one.

"Sir," said Sky, "as I see the Ky ideas, they are so simple that anyone with a little curiosity can be on intimate terms with them. As I understand it, the citizens of the Colony simply wish to be left alone."

Parliament's troubled outburst clearly stated that many of them disapproved of so benevolent an interpretation of their enemies' intentions.

Sky strained to see whether Firemaker had yet arrived. His desk still looked unoccupied.

President Lightman addressed Parliament. "Now you see another of the reasons I asked this particular young man to appear here. He has been to the Colony. He studied there. He has friendships there. As a trusting man of the Faith, he has compassion for them. Let me remind you that when others in his student group chose to make their lives in the new land, Sky Tinsmith chose to return to us, to his home, where he is needed. Therefore be generous to him. He can speak as an advocate for our adversary; and for us to learn the truth, we must consider ideas we instinctively abhor. Kindly avoid, therefore, outbursts such as the one we just heard. Now, young priest, answer me this: Have you read the essays of this rascal Infidel?"

"I have."

"Though you knew possession of such papers to be a punishable offense?"

"Yes. Sir, I am quite uncomfortable being here as an advocate of anarchy—"

"Chaos."

"Chaos, then. But there is one attribute of their philosophy I will advocate. The anar—chaotics advocate freedom of information. It is their theory that only an individual can judge facts; they therefore eschew authority in matters of conscience. I agree with this—not so much as it pertains to religion, not so much as a political stance, but as a scientific principle. I may take the Government's word for it that Ky is a criminal society, but unless I have seen it, I cannot know. I may have faith that Parliament will forever dictate human behavior in the minutest detail, but unless I have considered alternatives, myself, I cannot know. If the Ayatsport Press were allowed to publish Infidel's essays, and the most erudite opponents of them were asked to argue against them in print, then our people could decide. As it is, everybody knows the essays exist, but few know their contents. Furthermore, most of those who do read them do so precisely because they are forbidden. Forbid something and you make it desirable. I suppose that those who feel dissatisfied with the world will be drawn toward Infidel's ideas; and those who feel comfortable with their lives will shy away from them. And it's feelings, not knowledge, that breeds animosity and violence."

"Hear hear!" said someone, and there was a smattering of applause. Sky thought this voice sounded like the young representative, the toad, from Stormsville.

The President asked smoothly, "I take it you're in sympathy with Infidel."

"You may take it that I do favor freedom of information for all people," Sky said easily, pleased with his choice of words.

Every face in the Central Committee was a familiar face. One of them, a woman Sky knew to be Leaf Potter, asked him: "Will you share with us some of your observations of life at the Colony?" Sky thought the woman regal, handsome, with unfriendly eyes.

"I'll be happy to," he said, "but you must remember that it has been several years since I was there. Ambassador Harvester should be—"

"He will be asked," Leaf Potter said impatiently.

"Even when I was there, government was scarcely visible. I attended their Parliament once, and it was something of a farce. During it, they abolished some agency or other, and the ex-minister of it rose and quite genuinely thanked the members for sending him back to his farm. They seemed to treat the whole event as a joke.

"They certainly have not solved all social problems. The matter of charity concerned me most. Some poor fellow with no friends and nothing to offer would get little if any assistance. And there's the problem of religion. It has been rumored that the culture is largely atheist; and I'm afraid there's truth in that. The people frightened me a bit. I felt I could not predict their actions because I had no idea what they believed in."

"Were you treated badly?" asked President Lightman.

"On the contrary, I was treated like visiting royalty." Sky laughed. "That plus my innate suspicions of their motives left me feeling a little guilty."

Another member of the Central Committee, Nightsun Grocer, a withered old man with a high voice, interjected, "But surely, without communal motives, there has been no material progress to speak of. Aren't they largely an agrarian culture?"

Sky paused—not because he had no answer but because he was astonished that a member of the Central Committee could be so uninformed. "They have no cities the size of Ayatsport, but they are materially quite advanced. This might sound an almost treasonous statement; but I must tell you that when a man can profit in direct proportion to his labors, he labors more—not less."

Silence in the Glen suggested that many did, indeed, consider the statement treasonous.

Leaf Potter asked, "With no religion, have they any art? What of their architecture? Is Nyasport a city of mud huts?"

"Haven't you seen pictures of—?"

"Answer the question."

"Yes, they have art. I suppose we'd call it plain. The architecture, for the most part, is stark, but extraordinarily utilitarian. Nyasport has some buildings taller than—"

"And their weapons?" President Lightman broke in.

"Sir?"

"Can this, this great technology they seem to have be turned to weapons manufacture?"

"I don't—"

"Are they preparing for war? Is such a possibility within their philosophy as you understand it?"

"If—if they wished to, they could defend themselves effectively, I imagine."

"If they wished to?"

"Sir, what would a war against us gain them?"

"A World to dominate, to impose their will upon."

"But anarchy cannot wage war aggressively. There isn't the organization for it."

"Chaos."

"All right, *chaos* cannot plan a war."

"Chaos is by its nature a form of war—rebellion against any and all authority." The President took a deep breath and signaled for a page to bring him a pitcher of water. "Now let's lend your testimony some continuity, Sky Tinsmith. It has occurred to us that chaotics bent upon subverting the standing Government might seize upon Conclave as an opportunity for violent action. I grant you it's a matter of opinion who is behind the recent violence; but let's say *whoever* the perpetrators might be, will they use the superstitious fears associated with Conclave to accelerate their activities?"

"I'm afraid that's a logical possibility."

"Thank you. We appreciate the enormous courage you have displayed here today, and the information you have supplied. Please return to your desk, but stay ready to be called upon again. We ask that you keep yourself at the disposal of Parliament for the next several days at least. Are you comfortable in our dormitory?"

"Perfectly; thank you."

"Will the Clerk of the Glen please call Sergeant Miller of the West Borough Police."

Stepping down from the Witness platform, Sky stumbled. It may be that few guessed it was more from weak knees than from an inability to see clearly.

Taking his seat, Sky heard a voice he had heard once before—from his hiding place in a printing press. The man was saying:

"We were tipped off as to the warehouse's location by a woman whose name is being kept confidential for reasons of her safety." He went on to describe his plan of attack and its execution. "There wasn't much resistance." He was quizzed at length concerning the leader of the cell. "Arrogant bastard. Calls himself River. Never met anyone quite like him. He put up with the routine tortures, and, you know what? he kept trying to put *us* at ease. Said he knew we were just doing our jobs."

"The Ayatsport Press has identified this River as Infidel. Are you satisfied that this is true?"

"I'm not so sure. This River is smart, but I just can't see

him turning out all those intellectual papers."

"You've read Infidel's essays?"

"Had to. In order to interrogate him about them. He seemed to know some parts by heart, and others he got all wrong. He claimed he'd gladly admit it if he was Infidel. Said he might as well go out as a martyr and do a little good that way, as long as he was going to die anyhow."

The President scratched the back of his neck, then licked his lips thoughtfully. "Is he in good enough health to be brought here for questioning?"

"Here? To the Glen? I guess so."

"You mentioned electronic equipment seized at the warehouse. Have you traced its source?"

"It was taken from storage at the Spaceport."

A gasp of disbelief echoed around the Glen.

"Spaceport storage," the sergeant repeated. "We suspect somebody inside the Space Organization is in with them. That's being looked into now."

"How much of the missing equipment was found at the warehouse?"

"Not much. There's lots more of it around someplace."

"Thank you, sergeant."

There followed a string of Witnesses reporting on alleged violent activity on the part of the chaotics. It may be that Sky Tinsmith was the only one keenly seeking an alternative theory—some pattern, some bits of evidence that would lay the blame elsewhere. And patterns began to emerge for him. That the activity seemed confined to Ayatsport could have meant two things: that it was directed at Government, as Parliament assumed, or that it was being carried out by a strictly local agency. Maybe both were true. Never had an apprehended perpetrator admitted his guilt—suggesting the chaotics had been framed, cleverly, deliberately; while many of them, under interrogation, had admitted sympathy with Infidel's ideas—suggesting that the perpetrators knew where to find anarchists to blame. There was a rough geographic spiral of violence, narrowing on the Palace; indeed, there might be a bomb in the Glen; for the last three acts had been inside the Garden of Gods. If so, there had to be accomplices in Government itself. Sky remembered the woman's incredulous question that night at the warehouse: "You can't think that Parliament is committing murders just to have something to blame on us!" And he thought of Firemaker's quandry: "I'm beginning to see conspiracies in trivialities."

Why had Sky been called to testify during a time when Firemaker would be absent? President Lightman had made it seem an innocent enough coincidence; but if he had wanted to spare the hero embarrassment... if he had expected Sky to give himself away... if he already knew Sky Tinsmith was Infidel....

Conspiracies in trivialities. What were all those hastily scribbled notes passing via messenger to and from the President?

"Will the Clerk of the Glen please call the administrator of World Commerce."

During this man's testimony, Isle Firemaker arrived quietly and sat at his desk; he turned toward Sky and subtly raised his illuminated hand in greeting.

"... and some of the items have been dated," said the Witness. "There's no doubt that imports are still reaching us from the Colony, even though the Spaceport has been all but closed since the *Monz* landing."

"What sorts of imports?"

"Illegal items—hallucinogens, electronic components, a number of cases of books and periodicals, precious stones."

"Then Ky ships have been landing somewhere on World?"

"That's possible, but—"

"What's the alternative?" Another message was slipped into the President's hand.

"Protector. We know his smugglers operate a ship or two, but we've never located his base."

The President filed the note in a folder with the others.

"Thank you. You may return to your desk. Sky Tinsmith?"

He leapt to his feet, spilling papers. "Sir?"

"Please be prompt for tomorrow's session. I want you to assist in the interrogation of the traitor called River."

Sky paled; River would recognize him. "Certainly," he said.

The President continued hastily. "We've received word from Nyaslight Observatory that acceptable line of sight has been reestablished with Ky, and from Ayasport Broadcasting word that static with some indication of signal is coming from that direction. Forest Singer's transmission may be imminent. I am going to ask in a moment that the Glen be cleared in very orderly fashion so that a thorough search can be conducted for explosive devices. We will reconvene after the supper hour to listen to the criminal's tirade and discuss it afterward in an informal meeting. It seems certain that the broadcast will be a continually repeated recording; so timing will probably not be critical. Will the trumpets kindly sound the Recess?"

CHAPTER TWENTY-ONE

Night Of The Black Balloons

Nxo was a bright evening star, and the Galactic Edge was a luminous rim on the southern horizon; but the night was dark. Nya would rise with Ayat at dawn; Monz would not rise until after midnight. Conditions favored the agressor—a squadron of shadows which would bombard Ayatsport with words. This night the maelstrom of ideas over the Capital of the World acquired a personality; this night the vortex spoke.

Too soon after the setting of the suns, a dark round shadow became visible in the twilit sky. A projectile tracing a yellow line rose up and ripped into the black hydrogen bag. This scout disappeared in a puff of fire before transmitting a word.

But then they came in numbers and were detectable only as they eclipsed the stars. The fleet trusted to the wind and traveled in silence but for their chorus of one voice.

Forest Singer's words were low and slow and confident; it seemed to many that there was a smile behind them. It was a voice that had to be listened to:

"We have resorted to drastic measures to bring this message to you because your Government feels obliged to do your thinking for you, and this often means withholding the truth. Here are some truths we will not permit them to withhold:

"The citizens of the planet Ky have asked to be granted independence from political control by World Government. It is we, not your Parliament, who have suspended commerce until our sovereignty has been acknowledged.

We wish to take no hand in the running of World; and we wish no hand taken in the running of our own lives." Perceptive listeners heard what first might have seemed a burst of static but which, on closer listening, was applause; Forest Singer spoke before an audience on his planet. "Ignoring ethics and politics, surely it can be seen that this request is both logical and practical. We are so distant from you that no real administration is—or has ever been—possible. We are not linked even by conventional lines of transport or communication. Should any of you wish to respond to my words, your reply would take over an hour to reach me—be it a paragraph or a simple yes or no; the same for my answer to you. Making us answerable to your Parliament is not only unfair to us, it is meaningless to you.

"Yet we have no desire to isolate ourselves. World has products we wish to buy; we have products, far more than you are aware of, with which to balance the trade. But our freedom is more dear to us than your agricultural items, medical supplies, objects of art, and so on.

"Our ancestors all came from your World, but we have developed along very different lines. In many ways we are not like you now; we are a different kind of people. Listen to the man you call Infidel and brand a criminal. He understands our politics—a voluntary, peaceful society, our ethics—based upon a reputation for honesty, our epistemology—each man's determination of his own truth, and our dream—personal happiness through responsibility and accomplishment. Listen to Infidel when he tells you that the violence perpetrated in the name of anarchy acts against, not in favor of, our interests. In a free culture, violence is a dread disease: it stimulates governmental restraint, a restraint which can lead to forms of slavery the citizens can grow to accept as the norm—as has happened on your planet.

"Ingenious acts of nonviolence, however, such as the penning of essays containing revolutionary thought, such as their distribution by courageous men and women, such as the engineering of the balloons which tonight carry my voice—bring Nya's light to the darkened corners of your world. The activists involved in this movement are the

World citizens to whom we erect monuments. I am speaking to you now from a new theater in Nyasport, wholly owned by a cooperative of our citizens. The theater is called The Infidel." This time the interruption of applause was unmistakable; it was a cheer for Infidel.

"The people of Ky retain a fondness for our ancestors and a respect for the potentials of the people of World. We want to continue in your friendship. I have the support of the vast majority of our people in the plan I now propose:

"Let us meet face to face and work out our differences. Let a delegation from Ky, headed by myself, meet a delegation from World, which I propose be headed by Isle Firemaker. Let each of us gather several associates, who represent differing viewpoints, and meet on some neutral ground to seek a solution that can be recommended to all. By radio, such a dialog would take years; face to face, with good will and benevolent expectations, we might succeed in a matter of days.

"Our first thought was to suggest a rendezvous in neutral space between our systems; but we decided that achieving such pin-point accuracy in locating an unmarked region in the void would introduce unnecessary dangers. Further, unnecessary trust would be called for, as meetings would have to occur on one ship or the other. The depot at Syrdo would be acceptable to us, but it is inoperative; and still meetings would have to occur aboard a ship. We suggest, therefore, that we meet at the depot on Ru, Nya's intermediate planet. We eagerly await your reply to our proposal.

"Under normal circumstances, Ayatsport Press would carry no transcript of this message—only their estimate, based on Government policy, of it. We hope that the public nature of this event, however, encourages them to report factually. In any case, you will know whether they have done so; for you have heard the broadcast yourselves. You know the truth."

At the completion of the message, there was a sizzle of static; then a recording of the message was repeated again and again.

The streets were as congested as if it were midday.

People listened. The balloons increased in number; for every one spotted and shot down, two took its place. Hooks on dangling lines anchored the balloons to buildings and stilled their movement against the stars. A few daring souls took the lines and reeled in the loudspeakers; at those places, Forest Singer's voice reverberated from within the streets themselves. Arc torches blazed from the docks, the Spaceport, and the airdromes, to locate the invaders; and rockets occasionally punctuated the message by turning a hydrogen bag into a dissipating cloud of flame. Although there was no great physical danger, only intellectual danger, the city was under siege: the arc beams, the rockets, the bursts of hydrogen, the voice that wouldn't be stilled.

At dawn, anchor lines were cut on the remaining now-silent black bubbles, and the conquering shadows floated with the east breeze downriver, over Stormsville, and out to sea.

CHAPTER TWENTY-TWO

The Congress
Of Ky—Third Session

After deliberating throughout the previous night, Parliament reconvened for a short mid-afternoon session.

"We are in agreement on a number of points," the President summarized at the start. "Ayatsport Press must reprint every syllable of the rebel's speech, and our finest minds must dissect it word for word to uncover the duplicity, the ulterior motives rampant in every sentence of it. Along with the transcript and the analyses, highlights of the testimonies from yesterday's Parliament, concerning acts of violence attributed to the chaotics, will be published.

"The Cathedral will be asked to prepare a paper condemning the atheists and their campaign against us; political economists at the University of Ayatsport will begin work on a series of articles on the insanity, the impossibility, and the danger of life without Government; and the World Defense Organization, returned to active status, will begin preparing releases extolling the military superiority of World forces. Efforts to apprehend local troublemakers in sympathy with the criminals must be redoubled, of course.

"Since Firemaker seems to feel it might help, we will go ahead with plans for the meeting suggested by Forest Singer—to assure our people that every avenue is being tried in our efforts to resolve the matter of our errant tribe. But it must be assumed that Singer's invitation is an invitation into a trap; and all sensible precautions must be taken to insure the safety of Firemaker and those we assign to accompany him. The Colonial depot on Ru is unacceptable to us as a meeting place. The consensus at present is that Forest Singer and his party must come to World to say whatever they have to say.

"These and other issues are for our immediate attention. We must temporarily set them aside, however, because at this session we have available for our scrutiny the rebel calling himself River. We must see him now or not at all; for his execution is scheduled for an early hour tomorrow.

"Will the Clerk please call the prisoner and the priest Sky Tinsmith to the Witness platform." Exhaustion seemed to have depleted President Lightman's good humor. His expression said: Let's get this over with. "I'll ask Committeewoman Leaf Potter to assist in this. Are the technicians ready?"

Sky reached the platform first. Two tree-stump stools had been placed in front of the Witness chair; Sky stood beside one of them and watched as guards led in a tall man hooded in red. They were followed by a man lugging a machine of some sort. The hood, Sky thought, might be a salvation of sorts; River would not see him and might not recognize his voice.

"Please instruct me, President Lightman," he asked. "What do you hope I'll accomplish?"

The President nodded to Leaf Potter, who answered: "We believe you are more conversant with the ideas of Infidel than most. We'd like to know with certainty whether the man to be executed in the morning is Infidel or just a petty criminal. Any information leading us to others of the chaotics, or the real Infidel, will be most appreciated."

There was a curious exactness in the woman's voice, Sky thought, something that demanded precision, something more mechanical than human.

River was seated on the stool facing Sky Tinsmith.

The man with the machine was met by an assistant—who attached electrodes to River's wrists and chest and forehead. The machine operator dealt with the wires from them, while the assistant approached Sky. "Please open your shirt," he said in the manner of a doctor speaking to a patient.

Sky came close to fainting.

President Lightman said, "Standard procedure in criminal matters. You are being wired to a lie detector."

"But I'm the questioner!"

Leaf Potter said condescendingly, "It is painless."

Sky bared his chest and extended his wrists.

"We're ready," the machine operator announced finally.

Leaf Potter nodded to the assistant technician, who suddenly, with the flourish of a cabaret magician, whisked off River's hood.

"Do you know this man?" Potter demanded loudly. There was no way to know whether she addressed River or Sky Tinsmith.

Neither man answered—aloud.

"I have readings," the machine operator said.

"You may proceed, Sky Tinsmith," said the Committeewoman.

River smiled faintly. This triggered a state of mind Sky had been on the verge of assuming, that of absolute peace. It was the peace of the dying, the tranquility of knowing there was no course of action available, nothing left to do, nothing left to hide. The young priest had felt this before, and he would feel it again; but this was the only time he allowed himself to enjoy it. When fear might have overwhelmed him, he was unafraid.

"Hello," said River.

"Hello," said Sky, returning his smile. "Are you Infidel?"

"Yes," River said; and there was a murmur of surprise through the Glen. "We are all Infidel," River continued, "and Infidel is all of us. Did I write the famous essays of liberation? No, I haven't the intelligence or the wisdom. I only advocate their truths. It is easy to advocate greatness; it is like advocating sunlight."

Sky wiped his eyes and asked, "Were you responsible for the black balloons that spoke last night?"

"Exciting, wasn't it? I wrote the instructions for their manufacture; others printed and distributed them. Many people made balloons."

"Can you give us their names?"

"I don't know most of them. The names I do know will

be buried with me tomorrow. They will keep me company."

"Do you know the identity of Infidel?"

"Infidel has no other identity. You do not ask for Ayat's other identity; you do not ask for Infidel's."

The machine operator reported, "No false readings."

Leaf Potter handed papers to the assistant, who gave them to River and Sky. "Question him about this, Tinsmith," she said.

The paper was the last essay Infidel had written, in which he confessed his inadequacy, his failure, and his conviction that he was about to be apprehended.

Again without specifically directing her question to one man or the other, Leaf Potter asked, "Have you seen this paper before?"

Neither man answered.

The machine operator scribbled a note and handed it to Potter.

River took longer to read the paper than Tinsmith. The rebel at last looked at Sky and whispered. "This is not true." More loudly, he said, "This is a forgery. It was not written by Infidel; look at the small size of the signature symbol."

"I thought," said Potter, "that it bore quite a stylistic resemblance to other essays I've read recently—some attributed to Infidel, some not. Do you agree, Sky Tinsmith?"

"I don't know," he said.

"We have a reading," the operator reported.

"It is my personal conviction," said Potter, "that chaos and civilization are incompatible. Do you agree, Sky Tinsmith?"

"Yes."

The operator shrugged.

"That *anarchy* and civilization are incompatible?" asked Potter.

"We have a reading," said the operator.

"River—have you seen this essay before?" she persisted.

"No."

"Tinsmith?"

"No."

"We have a reading."

"Sky Tinsmith, do you know the identity of Infidel?"

"No."

"We have a reading."

"Sky Tinsmith, are you Infidel?"

"No."

"We have a reading."

Sky peered out into the gloom of the Glen. He saw Firemaker, his white hair glowing green in a decorative light, standing beside his desk. Sky said to his scarcely breathing audience: "Isle Firemaker is as shocked as the rest of you. He knew nothing of this."

"That reads true," the operator said.

President Lightman leaned forward and said, slowly, "Hold Sky Tinsmith in confinement without access to legal assistance, without visitations, without necessity for trial, without necessity for further sentencing, and prepare him for immediate execution by express order of this—"

An ear-popping concussion cut him off. Pieces of metal trees and vines rained down on the Glen, and a gagging dust descended from the source of the blast: high over the Knoll.

In the ensuing panic, someone—it might have been the assistant lie-detector technician—dropped a scrap of paper into Sky's lap. Handwritten in bold strokes were the words: "Grill, ceiling, directly behind Knoll."

"Be orderly," the President shouted into his microphone; "the damage has been done."

But just then there was another blast, this one near the floor. From it rose a billow of dust that reduced visibility to zero in its vicinity.

Sky stripped the electrodes from himself and River, grabbed the bewildered rebel's hand, and—as everyone ran for the Gateway—charged in the opposite direction.

A third bomb blew a hole in the stained-glass dome and sent down a hail of deadly splinters; but by then the Glen was empty.

CHAPTER TWENTY-THREE

Escape

The grill, which was easily removed, covered a hole that allowed warm air—and Sky and River—to escape into the atticspace.

The fugitives carried no batterylight or tools. River was barefoot and had nothing but the gray pocketless prison pajamas he wore; Sky, having shed his robe, wore casual clothes that fitted him rather well for the task of shinnying an iron tree—but he carried only his worthless identity papers.

The ancient structure was riddled with tiny breaches in its lath and plaster shell. Eventually, Sky and River perceived that they were between the lungs and ribcage of a monster. Gargantuan wooden trusses arched over them and descended at either end to blackness.

"Infidel," River whispered, pointing; "what's that?"

It looked like a large man standing on a beam not two meters away.

"Who are you?" Sky called softly.

It did not speak or move.

River extended a hand toward it, waved the hand; still it did not respond.

"Can you reach it?" Sky asked.

"It's too far. I'm afraid I'll fall through the shell if I stand on the shell. Wait...I see a metal strap." Something creaked when he put his weight on it, but he felt nothing give way.

Sky watched as his new friend struggled briefly with the menacing shape. The only sound associated with the enterprise was an odd rustling.

"What is it?" Sky asked impatiently.

"A bear suit, hood and all. For you, I suspect." He returned and laid it on the massive rafter at Sky's feet. "You're obviously being guided... or manipulated."

"Do you know who planted the bombs?"

"No. Don't you?"

Sky shook his head. "It's hard to believe anybody could do such a thing."

"I can believe it. Those bombs were part of your escape plan, had to be; the timing was too perfect."

"I thought of that."

"Shhh!"

There were voices coming from somewhere.

Sky and River lay against the rafter, scarcely breathing, and listened to vocal scraps of a search transpiring in the Glen below them.

"... hiding in here, it could take us days to look behind every bush and bolder... look at this mess... get the work lights on... kill them or capture them?... maybe got out in the confusion at the Gateway, slipped through with the others... make sure... guards at every level and every exit... call in the Ayatsport Police to give us a hand patrolling the Garden... get some more help in here, and the maintenance people..."

Sky whispered: "How do you suppose they got the suit up here?"

"That's the idea," River approved; "now's the time to think this through. I just realized that the bombs had to have been planted against the shell from this side. That's why they turned up nothing when they searched the Glen. Could have been done weeks ago."

"Then whoever it was knew I'd be arrested."

"Maybe they even—" River stopped mid-sentence.

"What?"

"Arranged for you to be found out. Don't ask me why; I'm just trying to consider everything. Let's get out of here."

"Now? With all those—"

"Yes, *because* of all those people down there. They're making so much noise they probably won't hear us moving. If we wait, they might get quiet. And pretty soon now, they'll start studying the gaping holes in the shell; then Palace Police will be swarming up here like rats. I wish we had a rope."

"And a ladder and a getaway plane," Sky mused. "Why don't we start over there where the suit was and try to guess what our benefactor expected us to do from there."

"That's better than anything I've come up with—which is nothing."

It was brighter in the atticspace now that work lights had been turned on below. River reached the spot first.

"You won't believe what's here," he said, lifting the rope that was tied to the base of the vertical support where the bear suit had been hanging. "Don't know how I missed it before."

"Does it lead down, by any chance?"

"Yeah, but I'm sure it's not by chance. It has knots in it. Good as a ladder. Can you make it down carrying the bear suit?"

"I'll tie it around my waist. Suppose there's a plane at the bottom?"

"No more talking. We're getting too far apart. There're some spikes here; don't let the suit get caught."

The muffled voices from within increased as did the intensity of light spilling through the shell, as the subjects of the search made their way down the steepening slope.

The slope became a vertical wall, then began to slant away from the climbers; they were dangling free over a darkness that contained, presumably, a floor.

Sky heard a voice from alarmingly nearby: "They caught the bomber—guy by the name of Weaver. Dressed in a maintenance uniform with a detonator right on him."

The rope suddenly jerked. Sky clutched it till his knees and knuckles ached. River had dropped to the ground, and the spring action of the rope had caused it to jump and then roll against the beam at the edge of the shell.

Sky became the weight of a pendulum—swinging helplessly across a great jagged opening in the shell. This must have been the location of one of the explosive devices. His repeated glimpses through the shell showed him an army of Police in the white light that dispelled the magic of the Glen and made of it a place both artificial and terrifying. The men were moving in a line down the tiers of desks toward the Knoll, directing their searchlights under every carved bolder and sculpted tree.

"Drop the bear suit!" River called incautiously.

Inside the Glen, someone said distinctly: "Did you hear that?"

Another voice: "I thought I saw something—up there on the wall."

The first voice: "God's alive! Look at the size of that hole. There! Did you see him?"

Sky never picked out the forms that owned the voices; because of the bizzare acoustics of the spherical shape, they might have been standing anywhere. He struggled to loosen and drop the suit while not losing his purchase—as the pendulum lost momentum.

"Now jump... jump!" River ordered him after the suit had made a soft thud below.

Sky scrambled down the rope—away from the hole that framed him, singled him out more effectively than a spotlight—but he hadn't the nerve to let go and fall until he heard gunshots and saw plaster imploding around him. He fell into soft dirt; River caught him as he toppled over.

The bulky costume draped over one shoulder, River tugged Sky toward the steps leading to a nearby catwalk. "It leads in only one direction," River explained, gasping for breath, "so I guess your rescuer meant us to find it."

Sky was grateful but too breathless and scared to utter a syllable.

The gunshots had stopped, but the great eggshell rumbled as Police stampeded back toward the Gateway. Suddenly the work lights over Sky and River winked on, and the towering beams, trusses and buttresses appeared as a leaning city made of rotten timbers—in which the streets were catwalks suspended on chains with links like fists; and the stars above were floodlights.

The dust was so thick it was slippery, but there were prints in it: someone had been on the catwalk ahead of Sky and River. The handrails creaked when they fell against them, and filled their palms with splinters.

The trail led them around the curvature of the Glen, behind the Knoll end. They were out of sight when their pursuers entered from near the Gateway; from their mingled shouts and scuffling, it seemed there was an army of them.

"Slow down!" River commanded hoarsely. He had perceived that the catwalk was coming to a dead end.

"The footprints keep going," said Sky, looking down.

At this point, the walk was suspended a good twelve meters from the ground; the bulge of the Glen, on their right, squeezed the walkway almost to a towering straight rock wall, on their left—an ancient wall that, a level or so higher, had boarded-over portals and windows. Just beyond the squeeze, the catwalk ended in mid-air. There was an old wooden ventilation duct girdling the Glen, and it seemed obvious that this catwalk had been placed to provide access to it. Sky and River stopped where there was a large gap in the duct—a possible avenue of escape.

"The footprints pass it by," Sky insisted. "Besides, the duct can only lead us back inside the Glen."

"Look at that—" River pointed. A little farther along, on their left, a single square block was agape in the rock wall. There was an opening. But the footprints continued beyond it.

River muttered, "I suppose we could be expected to climb the chains at the end. Or jump off."

"We have to find out," Sky said.

At the end of the walk, they looked up and saw that a hatchway to the roof was wedged open, near the top of the chains.

From sounds reaching them, it was evident that the search party had split in two and was approaching from both sides of the Glen; there were occasional shouted commands that echoed into gibberish.

River asked, "Which do you think—the old duct, the hole in the wall, or the roof?"

They both said at once: "The wall!" They had reasoned like lightning that they had three obvious choices, but if they could push the stone back into place, the Police would discover only two. They felt the planks beneath them vibrate suddenly: somewhere along the catwalk were moving feet other than their own.

River turned to run back to the break in the wall; but

Sky grabbed him. "Your footprints! You're barefoot!"

"Here—carry our friend," River said, relinquishing the empty bear.

Compared to Sky, River was a big man, but he jumped up onto the handrail with the agility of a child. Steadying himself with the support chains, he balanced like a circus performer and backtracked—while Sky walked backwards in the dust.

They imagined that the Police were split into two groups—one to search the roof, the other to thread their way through the length of the abandoned duct—but they never knew; for once their combined back and leg muscles had closed the stone, they heard no more from the cavity outside the Glen.

In the pitch darkness, River laughed oddly and said, "I just thought of that gruesome children's story about the boys who were too trusting and were led by a trail of candy into a dragon's mouth."

They saw their dragon's mouth in the beam of the batterylight Sky stumbled upon. It was an ancient room, a cube of about eight meters; it was lined with crudely executed tree-trunk marble columns, among which were jeweled mosaic murals that showed an ugly, misshapen, squat humanity dwarfed by the graceful insensate creatures of the wild; a swipe of River's bare foot revealed that the floor was covered with gold tile; the ceiling, black with soot, was a barrel vault of carved limbs and leaves.

There was a boarded door in one wall, a trap in the floor, and a chimney rising from a fireplace; it should not have been difficult to escape this exotic room. But it was clear they were to stay: in one corner there was a new air mattress, stacks of food cartons and water bottles (bearing the crest of the Palace kitchen), excrement bags (bearing Spaceport inventory numbers), a pile of spare batteries, and a stack of books. On the bed there was most of a human skeleton, arranged to look as if it were sleeping peacefully.

"I'll sleep well on a gold floor," River said. "The bed is for you. So is the food."

"We'll share everything; and the bed seems to be already occupied."

118

"We don't know how long the supplies have to last. I'm clearly not expected to be here. In fact, right about now, I'm supposed to be dying."

"We'll manage."

"There's only one bear suit."

Both men began to laugh—from the absurdities of the situation, from fatigue, from relief, from fellowship. They laughed as they cleared away the bones and inventoried the supplies—unable even to keep their volume low.

Just before they fell asleep (River commanded Sky to take the bed), River said, "That last essay of Infidel's is a forgery. You'll never convince me otherwise."

Sky grinned as he switched off the light. "I don't think I'll try," he said.

CHAPTER TWENTY-FOUR

The Benefactor

The first thing up through the trap in the floor, four days later, was a parcel; then a hand, then Merry Weaver's face.

Sky had deduced that she had to be somehow behind his escape; he was not shocked to see her; but never in his life had he come so close to being rendered senseless by the love that seemed suddenly to have replaced the blood in his veins.

"There's more food here. Eat it, Sky; you're going to need energy."

It was good that she dispensed with friendly greetings; Sky could not have replied.

"You're Merry Weaver?" River asked.

"Yes, and you're a pain in the ass. I didn't plan on having you to deal with."

"I was a dead man anyway. I'll do whatever you tell me to do."

Merry frowned when she saw Sky dividing his chunks of pork and beetroot with River, but she refrained from comment. She reached into a pocket, extracted a pistol, gave it to River, and answered his implicit question. "Shoot yourself if you're caught."

"River goes with us," Sky said.

"No," Merry said simply. "He stays here two more days, then tries to make it to the lowest level, to the sewers that open below the kitchens. He has a chance, a remote one."

River asked: "What would we have found on the roof?"

Merry tipped her head and smiled—a faint acknowledgment of his and Sky's perspicacity—and said, "I was afraid you'd try that. You'd have found many places to hide and numerous accessways to other parts of the Palace. But you'd have been caught, eventually."

"Where are you taking Infidel?"

"You don't need to know that. Sky—put on the bear suit."

"What was your reason for placing the bear suit on the shell," River asked, "rather than leaving it here with the other supplies?"

"Thanks for assuming I had a reason. That was my father's improvization—one that could have ruined everything. He thought there might be enough confusion for Sky to just put on the suit and walk out the door."

"That never crossed our minds," Sky said.

"Because there were two of you," Merry answered. "Let's get out of here; this is timed down to the split second. No—don't wear the head, stupid; carry it."

"Nice meeting you," River said without sincerity.

She shrugged. "Stay alive," she said as she lowered herself back into the floor trap.

Sky grabbed River's hands and squeezed them tightly. "I hope all the Gods will watch over you."

"And I hope," said River, "that all the anarchists will watch over you."

Sky and Merry retraced the history of civilization in their flight—from the darkness of the cave, through hallways of ever-increasing knowledge, to a door mass-produced of steel.

"Just outside that door," she said, "are rows of office cubicles for the individual members of Parliament. They'd never think to look for a fugitive there, and it won't be odd to see a bear ambling through. Head straight for the elevator at the end of the hall; take it down to the ninth level."

"What are you going to do?"

"Meet you there. I don't want us seen together. *Two* hidden personalities would be too close to what everyone's searching for. I'm going down on the maintenance elevator."

"But what do I do when—"

"You're scared. I can see it on your face. Don't be a sissy. Trust me. Now put on your headpiece and get out of here."

"All right. Merry, I've never seen you so—"

"Purposeful? Like it?"

"It makes you even more beautiful."

She laughed—warmly, Sky thought.

Merry had been right about the fact that others in the corridor would be wearing costumes; but she had neglected to warn him he might be the only one wearing the headpiece.

"And who is the ferocious black bear?" someone asked, teasing.

A man who was a frog from the waist down looked up from the water fountain where he'd been drinking. "One of our ladies, I'd guess. There's a smallish bear inside that big bad bear suit."

"Ah! An intrigue! The lady escapes from a rendezvous. We'll see who it was next year when one of our ladies returns with a little cub! Now who could have lent her that suit? What fat man among us has been appearing as a bear?"

"You know, that reminds me of a costume worn by... oh, but he hasn't served Parliament for a dozen years or more."

Sky was exuding gallons of sweat—both from fear and the heat of the furry suit—but he managed to muster a touch of humor as he waited for the elevator. He contrived a feminine pose and appeared to be daring them to guess "her" identity. When the elevator came, he waved a coy goodbye and almost enjoyed it when they laughed.

The ninth level was a boiler room where several workmen monitored dials as a consignment of fuel oil was being pumped in. It was a simple enough matter to remain unseen by ducking behind one of the mountains of machinery—where he found himself face to face with a snarling alligator, its jagged mouth gaping, its wings arched as for an attack. He stumbled back and nearly cried out.

"Control yourself," it said; "follow me."

Merry led him to a metal door that opened onto a circular staircase.

"Ever ridden a horse?" she asked as they descended.

"No."

"Then you'll have to learn the hard way." She reached into a pocket of her lizard suit and withdrew two more pistols. "Don't use this unless I tell you to," she said, handing him one. "And if I say shoot, obey me."

"I'm not sure I can."

"Sky, I like you; but I'll blast your head off before you get us captured. If I say shoot—you shoot. Now put the gun away."

There was only one attendant in the stable of parade horses. He was brushing a gallant young steed, whistling an old ballad, and seemed to be in no hurry to complete his job. "Well that's the smallest parade I've ever seen," he said to the approaching bear and lizard.

"We'd like," Merry said gaily, "to take two of your finest out for a constitutional."

The groom smiled. "Ah, two ladies then. May I see your authorization?"

Merry produced two plastic tokens. "I'm told these will suffice."

The groom studied them. They were pass-markers generally giving the bearer free access to Palace facilities. "I'm afraid I need more than these. Folks don't normally take ceremonial horses out into the Garden."

"No, but with the manhunt going on, the Garden is off limits to citizens; we'll have it practically to ourselves." She slipped a wad of money into his shirt pocket.

He gestured toward two horses which needed saddles.

Merry addressed Sky: "Why don't we give him a hand?"

"All right," Sky said in a high voice—again taking advantage of his small stature to appear female.

While tightening the straps, the groom said, "Don't you want to leave your animal suits behind? Hard to ride in those things."

"No," said Merry. "We're newly elected, and it feels good having them on."

This answer seemed to disturb the groom. "The

headpieces then. Please leave them with me."

"We'll keep them," Merry said firmly.

"I—I'm bound to ask you to remove them. With the criminals loose, no one is allowed to leave the Palace with their heads covered."

With startling speed, Merry drew her pistol and shot the groom dead. Then, as if she had done nothing more than sneeze, she hiked herself onto the horse and ordered Sky to do the same. "Before anyone investigates that bang."

At the arbor near Ayat's Tree, Merry invited the two guards there to step inside the mouth of the tunnel to examine her credentials.

"Shoot them!" Merry ordered.

Sky froze, and Merry killed them both. The reverberant explosions were so deafening Sky could barely hear her next command: "Slap that horse!"

Sky was both appalled at the killings and awed by Merry's nerve and decisiveness, her clear-cut sense of justice. A slap was unnecessary; Sky's horse followed Merry's into a gallop—eastward, straight across the Garden.

The poor beasts, ill-equipped for such exertion, flapped their limp wings pitifully and resisted Merry's blows and cries; but they covered ground. The Garden was essentially deserted. A group of workmen were operating a steam shovel, digging a grave off to the left of the route Merry took (a check of Palace records confirmed that this was to be the pit in which Merry's mother and father—convicted conspirators against the World—were executed the next day). All others on the grounds were dressed in green—Palace Police; but they were deployed mainly around the Garden's perimeter.

If there was a commotion developing behind them, Sky and Merry had no time to check it out.

Nearing the eastern border, Merry urged her steed into a jump over a low hedge. The animal flapped its wings furiously in mid-air. "Good boy!" Merry shouted. Sky's horse followed suit, and Sky fancied that the beast enjoyed the simulated flight.

They reached a seldom-used gate that opened onto a

back road. The gate was open; several guards lay dead around it.

Through the gate, across the dirt road, into Warrior's Field—with wild flowers knee-high to the horses, and a crocus revving its rotors.

"Gods alive!" Sky said to himself, "a plane!"

Warrior's Field is an unofficial park which, two hundred years ago, was constantly alive with military activity: this was the Palace's most vulnerable side, as well as its most effective alley of escape. Now the cannons and bunkers lay rusted and crumbled, covered with vines and flowers—a monument to the Peace of Unity. On this day, the few occupants of the field were citizens picnicking or out for a noontime stroll; they watched the mounted bear and alligator with passive interest.

The crocus motor whined up to speed as Merry and Sky approached it; it left the ground before Sky was fully inside the door. Merry pulled him in.

Lines on the ground converged toward the spot the plane had vacated as they shot into the air. Over in the Garden, Police were running toward the east gate. From the west, vehicles sent out from the State Airdrome bounded across the irregular landscape of Warrior's Field. They were all too late.

"How's our timing?" Merry asked Honor Townsman, the pilot of the crocus.

"It's going to be close."

"Good. It's got to be close, or we'll have no chance at all."

Sky had a recurring thought that, for the moment, drove away his growing list of questions; he said it aloud: "All those lives. It can't have been worth it. Besides, there's no place in the World I can hide—not now."

"That's true," Merry said.

The crocus was screaming at high speed southward—toward the Spaceport.

CHAPTER TWENTY-FIVE

On A Mission Of Conciliation

A lift-off siren wailed, and warning rockets burst overhead at regular intervals. A verbal countdown issued from an amplified system, but the fluttering of the crocus made it impossible to distinguish the numbers being read off. Sky and Merry shared a foot-strap at the end of the crocus strand; they swung, three hundred meters from the ground, toward the nose hatch of a titanic space-going whale poised for launch.

They were no longer carnivorous beasts but very small, very vulnerable human beings—reaching for the hand grips at the rim of the hatch.

They half-jumped, half-fell onto a clanging steel platform. Behind them the hatch shut like a vault door, and they could no longer hear the crocus, the rockets, and the countdown—only a chorus of humming machinery and electronics.

"Get below," snapped an unfamiliar, unfriendly voice. "Go to the second cabin level, take the two empty couches, and strap yourselves in."

Merry descended the vertical conveyor first; as Sky grabbed the passing hooks to follow, he asked the man in space-pilot green: "Who are you?"

The man answered reluctantly. "Friend Warrior, but my first name does not extend to you; I'm no friend of yours."

Descending through the pilot's compartment, Sky saw a familiar figure strapped into the commander's chair.

"Firemaker!" he said joyfully.

"I'm glad you're all right," the old man said; he was not smiling.

"Where are we going?"

"Eldry."

"Why?"

"It's the only neutral ground Forest and I could agree upon."

"But—Conclave—"

By now Sky was entering the next compartment down, where Sagacious Harvester continued the conversation:

"I thought you'd given up all that superstitious stuff."

"Harvester! Yes, I think I have; but if there's even the slightest gravitational disturbance, it'll be greatest at Eldry—the planet in the middle, the planet common to both systems."

Sky had recognized the middle-aged woman sitting, strapped down, next to Harvester. It was his interrogator from the Glen, Leaf Potter. There was a receiver within her reach; she turned up its volume as Sky reached the floor and continued downward, and Sky heard a voice saying: "... count at present is at least nine dead and seven wounded. Apparently the two chaotics disguised as Parliamentarians were both women, but Palace authorities have not discounted the theory that one of them might have been the escaped Infidel. The crocus in which they made their getaway was unmarked and was sighted heading toward...."

There were three acceleration couches in the next cabin down; Merry was fastening herself into one of them. Sky jumped into another. The third was empty.

"Who's in the cabin below us?" Sky asked noting that the conveyor descended further.

"A crew of three. I looked," she answered.

"Why are we going to Eldry? What are we doing here? Merry—what's going on?!"

Firemaker's voice sounded from the intercom: "Counting down from twelve...eleven...ten... nine...."

Merry smiled and reached over to take Sky's hand. "Everything will be clear to you by the time we reach

Eldry. We have a long trip ahead of us, hopefully not a lonely one."

This was a tenderness Sky had never known Merry to express. She was all possible women to him. "Merry, I love—"

"Don't worry if you pass out. They tell me many people do."

Sky was one of those who did. He felt a vibration that grew to teeth-jarring intensity; then came that sickening feeling in his chest and stomach he had felt when he let go of the rope ladder outside the Glen—only this time, he never touched bottom.

CHAPTER TWENTY-SIX

On A Mission Of Power

Following the departure of Firemaker's ship, there was an end-of-the-World quiet at the Spaceport; but it lasted only a few minutes. Soon another countdown commenced over the public-announce system, and rockets again rose to clear the airways.

The announce system marked "... minus seventy-four, seventy-three, seventy-two...."

In the terminal, the Chief Controller was trying to quiz President Lightman, who had just arrived by crocus from the Palace.

"You allowed them to get away?" the Controller asked.

"Well," the President laughed, "after doing our best to stop them, yes."

"Why didn't you abort Firemaker's launch?"

"Firemaker and I are old friends."

"But... he's carrying escaped criminals!"

"He's carrying political pawns."

"Does he know our ships are going to pursue him?"

"They're going to escort him."

"But—does he know about them?"

"Firemaker and I are old friends."

"Has war been declared against Ky Colony?"

"No."

"Then why all the munitions aboard the escort ships?"

The President of the World smiled enigmatically.

"I know—you and Isle Firemaker are old friends."

An hour later the ground shook again, this time with twice the violence as before, as two more ships of the World erupted simultaneously into the afternoon sky.

CHAPTER TWENTY-SEVEN

On A Mission Of Conquest

"Funny things, orbits," Protector mused late that night. "Leave a week later—arrive a week earlier, traveling at roughly equivalent speed. Clever fellows, those scientists."

Honor Townsman agreed. "It's because everything out there just keeps on moving," he said.

Protector and his stalwart were on their way via numerous modes of transport—at this time over the ocean in a crocus—to the World's only private, and secret, launch facility. (It's exact location still is not known, but it is believed to be somewhere in the great salt desert of the Continent of Flame, perhaps not very distant from the Oasis of Nxo.)

It was well past Nya's rising, and the sea seemed strewn with rolling blue diamonds. A sensual wind blew steadily through the open windows of the low-flying crocus.

"Merry got aboard all right?" Townsman asked.

"Indeed. I never doubted she could pull it off."

"But her father was arrested. What went wrong?"

"Nothing went wrong. Absolutely nothing."

Some time later, Townsman asked: "You're really going through with this whole thing?"

"What does it look like? You're on your way to Eldry, aren't you? Where's your sense of adventure, Townsman?" He laughed. "You think I've lost my mind, don't you?"

"It's not every day that I watch a man offer a planet to the woman he loves. I don't understand...what's your gain in this?"

"My gain, dear fellow, is the very planet I'm giving away."

Six days later, during a morning hour, a private space ship set off a white storm as it rose in thunder and fire out of the salt dunes.

CHAPTER TWENTY-EIGHT

Ky—Legacy Of Malefactors

To the ancients, Ky was Grace—a bright speck of light that passed to and fro across the face of the Goddess of Truth, dimming with humility upon approach, brightening with admiration upon retreat, endowing Nya with feminine sensibilities.

Friend Inventor saw Ky as one of three bluish spheres which exhibited phases—much as Ayat's inner planet, Nxo, changed shape with its seasons. The industrial minds of the Age of Awakening saw Ky as a planet of water and clouds—a potential garden ripe for exploring, ripe for annexing.

In 4041, the first Colonists—convicts and exiles—looked up past alien scrubby trees into an intensely blue sky, to the land of their birth: a tiny crescent barely visible within the atmospheric halo surrounding insignificant Ayat. The Gods had been turned inside out.

The pioneers looked into their new violet sky and laughed. The sound contained cynicism, contempt, relief, and the triumph of successful swindlers: they had contrived to be thrown out of prison into paradise.

When the first Colonial overseer—an appointee of World Government—insisted that their first efforts be toward erecting a church and that their second be toward erecting a Government House and jail, they murdered him.

Then they built private shelters and made weapons. *These* became their Gods and their Government.

The lazy among the pioneers either reformed or were left to perish. The vicious were defeated. The power-hungry were laughed at. The ignorant were taught by the skillful in need of cheap labor. The resourceful ascended. The men and women of Ky applied, of necessity, all the science of the Age of Awakening in their conquest of the alien environment.

On World they had sought absolute freedom of action—for which we labeled them criminals. In serving their sentence, they earned the very thing World had forbidden them: liberty.

Other shiploads of criminals—pioneers—arrived at Ky and were greeted with cheers, laughter, and open arms.

The children of the pioneers were not, for the most part, taught the ways of Syrdo and Ayat; they were taught a raw new ethic. They were taught by example that Nature was not a God to be catered to, but an enemy to be outwitted. They were taught that any man who lived as he wished to live, without endangering another man's living, was worthy of respect; and any man with a reputation for honesty was worthy of admiration. They were taught that generosity was no duty but merely a practical attitude, sometimes a pleasure. They were taught that the essence of depravity was the conviction that "society" ought to supply a man's wants—because for several generations there was no "society" on Ky, no abstract *them* from whom to expropriate another man's needs, only neighbors with names.

Of the love we claim to feel for all the Gods, and, by extension, for all of humanity, the inhabitants of the Colony have scarcely an inkling. Of the diversity of purpose they honor among themselves, we of World have very little understanding.

"Leave me alone and I wish you good fortune," is their common sentiment, their tradition.

World has not left them alone. We have attempted for generations to conscript their labor, to take their wealth, to prescribe their behavior, and to force our Gods upon them.

At last they ceased to wish us good fortune.

That, as the Colonists see it, is the foundation of the Ky rebellion.

CHAPTER TWENTY-NINE

The Children Of The Plague

On 3d-9m 4111 (translated to World's calendar) there occurred on the planet Ky a fairly ordinary event; but it was something impossible to see on World, something arising from a cultural context of which World is largely ignorant.

At Eye Valley Stadium, on the outskirts of Nyasport, principle city of Ky, an assembly of young men and women were in training for the Ky Athletic Exposition, to be held in conjunction with the city's centennial anniversary. This particular team of athletes commanded a considerable audience, even when they only practiced.

In the stadium's spacious parking lot were vehicles vastly unlike any found on World; hardly any two were alike. There were two and three-wheeled peddled cycles of every conceivable color and configuration, and motorized cycles in almost as great a variety. The "conventional" automobiles were generally wedge-shaped, and bore no resemblance to animals or fish of either Ky or World. There were folded kites strapped to tiny motors and larger flying contraptions that looked like crocuses with their decorative shells removed—nothing but machinery which was polished and painted in pretense of being its own decoration.

A keen observer might have witnessed a curious string of events. A young woman alighted; folded her kite, parked and locked it; and walked briskly, happily, toward the stadium entrance. Before she was out of the lot, a small crocus had landed, and one of its two male passengers had jumped out to follow her.

The woman took her place in the queue at the gate; but one of the guards dressed in the black of the Nyasport Safety Service evidently recognized her, and waved her in. The man, fidgeting, fearing he might lose sight of his quarry, attempted to push forward.

"You—wait your turn," a guard demanded.

The man removed a card from a sleeve pocket and thrust it at the guard. The guard read:

> COURTESY REQUEST
> Kindly extend cooperation to
> WOLF HILLSMAN
> Investigator on assignment
> KY PROTECTION ENTERPRISES
> Desert Circle 985
> NYASPORT

"Are you armed?" asked the guard.

"No," Wolf Hillsman said, lying. He carried a small dart pistol as did many Ky citizens of cities.

"Go ahead. Call on us if you need assistance."

"Not likely to," Hillsman said, hurrying ahead of the waiting crowd.

He hesitated in the carnival which serves the stadium as a lobby. Even on this practice day, tradesmen had opened their booths and sent out strolling salesmen; they offered snacks, telescopes (these were the hottest-selling items), recordings and books, firearms, and treacherous drinks and drugs. Wolf Hillsman hesitated because his woman had paused to buy a glass of spring water; similarly, he hesitated at a wine booth.

A commotion arose behind him at the gate. He stood on tiptoe to see over the heads of the crowd. A mob of red-uniformed men were demanding to be let in. He knew them to be guards from Ky Protection Enterprises, his own company.

"You have no invitations," the chief guard in black lamented, more to himself than to his antagonists.

"Yeah, but we outnumber you," said one in the red guard as he pushed his way inside.

A teacher (she stood with a cluster of youngsters) said to an adult companion: "The more I see of the red service, the less I like them. I'm going to recommend that our school switch to blue—or even black."

An approaching red guardsman overheard her and explained good-naturedly, "We're just off duty, lady, and want an hour of entertainment. Besides, if there's any trouble here, the black boys know we'll give them a hand."

Wolf Hillsman downed his wine in a gulp as he saw his woman proceeding into the stadium.

The stadium designer had built the bleachers in a perfect circle around a grassy field on which straight lines and circles accommodate many of the same contests we know on World—and several other games indigenous to Ky. The new games relate to the planet's gravitational attraction, which is .7154 that of World. The light gravity games require markers of such height that just looking at them a World visitor reels with acrophobia. The greatest of these is a metal pole supported by cabling and containing numerous protrusions and hoops; it is fully 285 meters high and can be seen from all over Nyasport and even beyond. It rises from the east end of the playing field, up past the four tiers of bleachers, past the entablature rimming the stadium, higher than the view of downtown skyline buildings, up into the blue-black sky. Highly reflective, the pole seems made up both of the darkness at the zenith and all the lights in the sky. It transmits the blue of Nya in blinding glints, the amber sparks of dim and distant Ayat, the smudge of red from the dull red dot of Monz, and the blue-gray of Ky's Eye of Night—one of its two satellites. (The Eye always hangs, in a synchronous orbit, like a protective lamp above the city. Tradition says that its position guided explorers to this coastal valley, where they established their settlement.)

It was an especially bright afternoon. The shining tower was raised in a salute to the illuminators.

Wolf Hillsman had no difficulty following the woman. She made her way along the sparsely peopled benches and thence to the sidelines—where she greeted some of the athletes engaged in limbering exercises. She waved to someone out near the base of the tower; when he returned her wave, there were scattered cheers from the scattered audience.

A visitor from World who happened to find himself among these spectators would be appalled at what he saw. His attention would at once be drawn to the team on the field. He would scarcely notice their attractive skin-tight electric-blue costumes, their wildly gymnastic exercises, their bone-thin bodies, or the balletic grace with which they moved. He would see only their wings, long batlike wings the color of sun-tanned skin, a sight no soul of World ever expects to see: adult human beings from whom the wings had not been removed, naked human wings advanced to maturity. An unspeakable depravity.

These were the Children of the Plague.

This they all were called, even though only a few of their number had properly earned the appellation. The senior members had been four or five years of age during the plague of 4089—during which all normal surgeries were suspended. By the time life had once again stabilized, several of the winged children had glided from rooftops, hilltops, mountaintops; they had learned that they could fly. Strange to say, some of their parents found their capability appealing, and left the decision concerning dis-winging to the children themselves. Many kept their peculiarity, at least through childhood; and some have kept it to this day. During the past score of years, other parents (unencumbered by the superstitions of World religion) allowed their children the same freedom. Thus the team of thirty on the stadium field ranged in age from 14 to 28.

It should not be assumed that mature wings are plentiful on Ky. Relatively few keep them; for except when airborne, a winged human is restricted in his movements by the appendages which, even though they fold in close when not in use, nevertheless inhibit physical activity. Further, a winged man must, even on Ky, keep his weight to a minimum and maintain strict exercises to strengthen wing muscles. Three children with inadequate physiques died, over the years, when their muscles failed them and, their wings torn by the winds, they fell.

Nor should it be assumed that a person with wings was considered freakish by the population of Ky. On the contrary, they were admired and valued with a passion approaching patriotism. They were a national treasure. They were admired not in spite of, but because of their unusual means of survival and their individualistic path to happiness.

Because the flyers were conspicuous, they were singled out for leadership. In addition to their fees and salaries as athletes, most of them augmented their incomes with honorary or actual positions in major commercial enterprises; and they were frequently to be seen advertising and endorsing inventions and products for sale. All of them were known to the populace by name.

Their captain was Forest Singer. It was he to whom the woman had waved—he who now motioned for the others to join him at the base of the tower.

He took a microphone from a bracket and said into it simply, "I'm glad so many of you could come; we love an audience. You'll see not only our familiar routines but a portion of the finale we're preparing for the Exposition. Remember that the Exposition will take place during dim hours, when only the Eye and Monz will be in the sky; you'll have to use your imaginations a bit today.

"You can earn your free admissions by filling in the criticism cards you will be given as you leave. And if you can think of anything that might add excitement to our show, please let us know. But we won't strap rockets to our backs or perform lewd acts in mid-air. Keep your suggestions practical—and polite."

Forest kept a small young man beside him and instructed the others to begin their ascent up the ladder of spokes that led to the 10-meter platform. "You've heard," Forest continued, "about the young man who has renamed himself Wingmaster—with no objection from any of us, incidentally. You have read about his courageous recovery from a fall last year and the experimental surgery he elected for himself: to have the humerus, radius and metacarpals of his wings replaced with hollow, lightweight synthetics. This removes him from competition, of course; but as you'll see today, it earns him the spotlight in exhibition flying. I want you to meet him now."

The youngster, several inches shorter than Forest and thin as a skeleton, took the microphone merely to say, "Thank you," to the applauding audience.

A man shouted from the bleachers: "Is Wingmaster replacing you in the Exposition?"

Forest answered candidly, "We still haven't received confirmation that Firemaker has lifted off. If he has, I've promised to go to Eldry with the peace delegation. I'd miss the Exposition."

The grumble from the stands said clearly that they considered the Athletic Exposition of greater import than the peace conference.

A woman shouted out: "Why Eldry, of all places?"

Forest answered, "Their guidance systems aren't as sophisticated as ours; they have to have a homing beacon—like the one still operating at the old Eldry base. We can talk about this later. Listen, the main reason I invited so many reporters today was to show you that the performance can transpire splendidly without me. You won't even notice I'm missing when Wingmaster starts his routine. For example—"

On Forest's cue, the lad with the lightened wings began to flap furiously. To the amazement of the spectators, he took to the air from a standing position—something none had seen before—and flew up higher than the 10-meter platform. At that level, he extended to a gliding pose and lazily circled his teammates—who were themselves applauding him.

On Wingmaster's signal, the team peeled off, diving and extending their wings, alternately flapping and gliding, dipping nearly to the ground, rising slowly, achieving lift. Forest was last off the platform; he joined his team in a circle over the heads of the delighted crowd. Laughing, he shouted down, "Try to imagine music! At the Exposition we'll have the entire Wheelright symphonic ensemble accompanying us!"

It was easy to imagine music. The thirty Children of the Plague soared and dipped in ripple and rhythm, rose in arpeggios and burst in crescendos. Forest and Wingmaster were joint conductors.

The wider the team circled, the higher they climbed. They teased and touched the great tower—as if to stress their independence of it. Higher—past the 40-meter mark, the 50, the 80, the 100, the 130. Spectators reached for their telescopes. The flyers were safer from miscalculation at such heights, but a snapped tendon, a cramped muscle, even exhaustion could mean death from a fall.

They began to alight on the tower at various heights; but Wingmaster continued to circle and climb. Not once had he touched the tower. The audience followed him up and up, to the tiny shelf at the very top, at 285 meters, where he finally folded his wings to rest. It's doubtful whether the shouts and cheers reached him as anything more than a faint rattle on the wind.

For an hour the team exercised their competition moves—plunging toward the ground, swooping up, having their dive lengths measured...tumbling with wings retracted, diving through hoops, gliding, accelerating, stalling, testing, measuring—all the while postponing the exhibition of Wingmaster who waited patiently at the top.

Suddenly, without preamble or announcement, there was a puff of orange smoke from the top, and the young star dived off like a swimmer and fell like a rock—down, down, down through a series of hoops—carrying the smoke-making device with him. Well below the 100-meter mark, he extended his wings, caught the wind, and soared up into an inside loop. The observers turned their gasps into shouts of approval. He seemed to be flying straight up—an optical illusion of which the aerialist knew how to take theatrical advantage—and then he was plummeting toward the bleachers.

He leveled out over the heads of all at a breathtaking speed—trailed by sound like a gust in a gale. He was grinning from ear to ear, and the crowd could hear his laughter. He tossed the spent smoke bomb onto the grass of the field and zoomed back into the sky.

Wingmaster had so commanded the audience's

attention that most were unaware that the rest of the team had made it to the top of the tower. There they were spiraled around the topmost section of the pole. All at once the pole bloomed like a flower as all wings extended—and it was a radiant blossom: the flyers had electric lamps of great brilliance strapped to their wrists. As they took to the air, long colored streamers trailed out from their feet. And a laser-light wheel of a thousand spokes formed a spinning canopy emanating from the tip of the tower. Even in bright daylight the effect was startling; in darker hours, it would be an overwhelming effect.

Wingmaster was ablaze with lights outlining his body, extremities and wings. He flapped up beyond the gliding flyers and hovered while they formed themselves in a circle. Gently floating downward, that circle, outlined in light and trailing long streamers, became a target for the incredible aerobat. Wingmaster dived through the circle, flapped back up, and dived again.

Forest Singer broke out of the circle and joined him for the last plunge, after which the team sailed loose and formed a straight line—which landed, running toward the tower, on the soft grass of the playing field.

Forest and Wingmaster were still in the air. They chased each other higher and higher and ended with multiple summersaults, in perfect unison, which brought them into a near-the-ground wing extension up to a gliding stall—and finally a feet-first drop to the grass.

The spectators were ecstatic. They rushed down the bleachers to the field fence, which many vaulted over.

The spell was shattered; the flyers were human again. They laughed and hugged each other, and happily accepted the embraces of the youngsters, guardsmen, reporters, friends and relatives—before they draped arms and wings about each other and headed toward the showers.

"May I have your attention, please?" asked a man's voice from the public-address loudspeakers. "We have just received word that Firemaker's party is in space, on its way to Eldry. Infidel is with him, and it is confirmed: Infidel is Sky Tinsmith."

Forest kissed Wingmaster on the forehead and said, "Well, the Exposition is all yours, my friend."

Wingmaster chuckled. "I won't let you down."

The woman who had been followed into the stadium called, "Forest!" from behind the field fence. Wolf Hillsman was standing practically at her side.

"Meet me at the gate!" he yelled back at her, and continued toward the locker rooms with his team.

CHAPTER THIRTY

Masters Among The Masterless

Forest Singer organized his first flying team when he was eleven. With seven other aerobats, of about that age, he toured the towns and provinces during the decade-long reconstruction following the plague. The team greeted rebuilders, most of whom had lost mates and loved ones, with signs of survival, talent, success, light-heartedness, promise, and evidence that not only would humanity prevail, it would even dare to fly.

It was often said on Ky that whenever Forest was not in the air he was off in the abstract world of books. He was ravenous for control over his own destiny. His childhood observations during the plague may have amplified this motive in him.

By the time he approached his twenty-sixth year, the time of the confrontation with *Monz* on Syrdo, he was regarded one of the most important men at the Colony. As a moderator, an objective sifter of personal claims and relative values, he had no equal—not even among the elders of Nyasport. He was also considered an engineer of exceptional talent. He was involved—as innovator or assistant—in the development of such technological strides as synthetic-fabric manufacturing machinery, atomic-plant safety devices, metal-alloy content monitors, chemical foams for fighting fires, and convenience devices beyond World's imagination—including machines that clean away dust by suction, ovens that fit into cabinets and cook by electric radiation, and mechanisms to maintain any desired climate in enclosed spaces. (These devices, we must stress, are common on Ky—in the possession of ordinary citizens!)

For each of these mass-produced items sold, Forest received a percentage payment. He was a wealthy man. Our people would have despised him for the very reasons the people of Ky loved him. He was a king without slaves, an authority without magic, a general without an army. On World, he simply could not have been allowed to mature.

Starlight Surveyor, who waited for Forest at the stadium gate, knew all these things. Furthermore, she thought of him as a man; and she loved him.

When Forest arrived, having shaken reporters in the locker room, Ayat had set; Nya was low, and the Eye was nearly at half-phase (phases of the synchronous sphere range from new at noon to full at midnight, daily).

"I didn't expect you today," he said, slipping his arm around her waist. "You've seen all that before."

Her glance said: I never tire of watching you. "Besides," she said, as if she had spoken, "I have things to tell you; one of them is that I'm being followed. See that man heading for the parking lot?"

"I don't recognize him."

"Neither do I, but he's a clumsy tail."

"Do you know why—?"

"I think so. Take me home with you. We can talk along the way."

They loaded her folded motorkite into Forest's four-passenger limousine—a chromium-sheathed flyer trimmed with blue-enamel lines—and climbed into the back seat. Forest instructed his pilot: "Take us home, Bumper," and the craft lifted instantly, its large rectangular rotors whining brittlely in Ky's mountain-top atmosphere. They struck a course away from the east-coastal city southward toward the Marches of Man.

Forest opened a window, and an icy wind rushed in.

Starlight closed it again; her look said: Are you *trying* to catch cold?

"If we're going to glide down, I have to get used to the air." He compromised by opening it partway.

Her expression of disapproval made him laugh. He

enjoyed the sight of her slim figure, the blue dress she had worn to honor his team, her light-brown hair that waved as if underwater in the faint breeze, and her clear, adoring eyes.

"Now be serious," she admonished. "If I'm right about why that man was following me, there might even be a listening device hidden in your plane."

"Bumper," Forest addressed the pilot, "did you leave the plane unattended at the stadium?"

"'Fraid so. I went in to watch your finale. But the lot was well guarded—by blacks *and* reds."

Starlight said thoughtfully, "I think they'll want to know if I'm going to break a confidence and tell you about the merger."

"Perhaps you'd better tell me nothing," Forest suggested. He was on hands and knees searching first beneath his chair then Starlight's—where he found a small metal box.

"They assume I'll tell you everything, so I might as well."

He gave her a look of warning, but not in time. She realized he was afraid she might endanger herself by talking, but it was too late.

Forest pried off the box lid and found inside the components of a pick-up and transmitter. He tugged two wires loose and tossed it onto the empty co-pilot's chair. "What merger?"

"Ky Protection Enterprises has bought out my father."

"What precisely did they buy?"

"Everything—facilities, records, methods, and our work force, though of course the men can quit if they want to. As of now, there is no more blue security police; and the red is the most powerful armed force in the history of this planet."

"Will your men quit?"

"I doubt that many will; their salary has been nearly doubled."

"Why do you suppose they care about confidentiality? Surely they can't expect to keep this quiet."

"I think they're afraid their very size will scare customers away. You'll still be seeing guards in blue—just as if it's still an independent service."

"Were you in on the negotiations?"

"Occasionally."

"Did they ever mention—?"

"Protector? No, but I'm more convinced than ever that he's the real owner of the red service. The spokesman had to get final authorization from their 'boss,' and that took several hours—as if they had to radio World and wait for a reply."

"Would your father have sold if he'd known?"

"I don't... well, yes. He's always admired Protector. I guess Father would like to think he'd have the guts and wits to live as a bandit under an oppressive government."

"Was their offer generous?"

"Very. Last week we had a company operating a shade below its profit line. Today, Father's a wealthy man. He'll stay on for a while as manager, then consultant."

"You're no longer employed, I take it."

"I quit. I wish I'd had a more crucial job than executive secretary. The company will run along without so much as a hiccup."

Nya had set, and out of its purple twilight rose an irregular sliver of a crescent, the other of Ky's satellites, the Rock. (This tumbling mountain orbits so close and so swiftly that it flies from west to east and makes two passes per date. The Rock gives Ky a calendar the rough equivalent of World's: as it first crosses the latitude of the Eye day begins; on its second pass, there's imaginary nightfall—no matter where the other lights of the sky may be.)

"Good evening," Forest said, noticing that Starlight too was watching the growing crescent.

She grinned; then her happiness faded. "There's something else I should tell you."

"Hmmm?"

"You didn't hear the full report concerning Firemaker's lift-off. Sky is with him. And so is Merry Weaver."

He looked away, out the window toward his mountaintop castle which was edged in moonlight. To judge by comparing reactions, this news jarred him more than the possibility that Protector could be setting himself up to be dictator of the Colony. "Why?" Forest asked dully.

"To see you again?" Starlight speculated.

"Well, I have no desire to—"

"Don't you? Then seeing her might help."

The plane was hovering over Forest's mountain. "Want me to land?" the pilot asked.

"No, this will be fine. Make a wide circle at, oh, twelve knots. Come on, Star, strap on your wings!"

At the open port, Forest said bluntly, "I've always been unfair to you."

She laughed. "Oh no, you've been so honest with me that I can't forget her either."

"That's what I mean."

"Jump, lover."

They soared from the plane—Forest with his natural wings extending, Starlight with her artificial rainbow-colored one fluttering in the icy wind—under the pale gray lights of the Eye and the Rock.

From above, Forest's home looked like a collection of flat boxes—their corners intruding upon one another—with some extremities reaching over the cliffs of the baren stony peak. There were smears of yellow-white light on the decking that zigzagged around the rectangles; these were from lamps inside. By World standards, it was palatial; three or four of our families could live there in comfort, even with measures of privacy. But the structure was stark, devoid of sculptured vines, blossoms or creatures—a foundation awaiting the loving hands of artisans.

The romantic eyes of Ky saw it as a nest for flying creatures.

As the limousine's sound diminished toward the city, the two flyers circled in a falling tightening spiral—like two scraps of paper in the funnel of a dust-devil.

CHAPTER THIRTY-ONE

Two Women, Half A Man

Forest left his bed. He assumed Starlight was awake; but she said nothing to him.

His body still hot from sex, his wings still tingling from the day's exertion, he slid open the glass portal and stepped onto the deck. The cold air was a welcome shock, but his wings involuntarily spread a little to shield his naked back.

Their love making had been illusory. He had been with two women, Starlight with only half a man. Merry Weaver's ghost had appeared between them. His hands could neither pull her closer nor push her away; they passed through her image. And only Starlight's body provided him heat and sensation.

Forest gripped the railing of the deck and stared toward the distant city where millions of lights twinkled in Nyasport's own waves of warmth.

Merry stood beside him, nonmaterial, invisible, whispering in his ear.

"A man with wings," she laughed, "the most exquisite affront to the World!"

"I mean nothing to the World," he said, remembering how it felt to float the palm of his hand over the flawless skin of her back. The conversation he was having with her memory was made up of a year's fragments.

"You mean the World's destruction."

"I only wish to pry its fingers loose from Ky."

"You'll end up cutting its hand off at the wrist. Ky is their errant child, their dependent cripple. They mean to love you into submission."

"They've tried that for a hundred years. It can't surprise the people of World to learn that we want to live our own lives."

"Surprise them? It will outrage them. They will think you ungrateful and immoral." She moved tight against his side and moved her hands over his wing shoulders, his back, his chest. "And when World Government falls, that shining city there on the horizon could be yours. Ours."

"I don't like jokes of that sort."

"Then I'll stop making them. I'll do—I'll *be*—anything you want."

"Nor jokes like that."

"Then I'll stop making them." She pulled him to the deck; she kissed his chest, his stomach, his penis. Her ghost vanished.

Forest stood alone in the cold air, sweating, sexually aroused. Love and hatred of dynamic, fearless, beautiful Merry Weaver collided in his soul with a great disapproval of his own youthful weakness; his heart raced. He mumbled aloud, "She wasn't joking," and came close to convincing himself of it.

CHAPTER THIRTY-TWO

An Eccentric In The Metropolis Of The Insane

From a distance, Nyasport looks like a collection of crystals in a green cushion at the edge of a table of sand.

The table is the equatorial desert stretching from the sea to another shore more than two thousand kilometers to the west. This natural streak of tan—broken here and there only by serpentines of mountainous rock—looks from space to be the result of a crude attempt to deliniate the planet's waist, as on a globe for study. Arrid though the area be, its warm climate, predictable (slight) rainfall, nearby (shallow) fresh-water ocean, and sea-level atmospheric pressure well qualify it for habitation.

The green cushion is made of vegetation, most seeds for which were brought from World. On Ky the trees are not sculpted, pruned, or even trimmed; they are allowed to spread and attain their full heights (often taller than their kin on World owing to Ky's gentler gravity). Among familiar greenery flourish cactus, grasses, wildflowers, vines, and "birch" trees native to explored areas of the Colony planet. Having no jungles to menace them, the citizens of Nyasport seem intent on creating their own. There are certain areas, near canals, which have even become too thick and wild for human passage. (These are, as you would imagine, places of adventure for children; but we once saw a grown man come to such an impasse, laugh delightedly, and proceed to thrash his way through it.)

The crystals in the landscape are the newer buildings, made of polished metals, glasses, and plastics. "That doesn't look like a city at all!" many a World observer would say. Another might opine, "It looks like a metropolis for the insane!" Yet another might say, "No wonder we call them chaotics!" Such observers would not yet have grasped the Ky mentality; they would be seeing Nyasport's impossible diversity through the eyes of World's community builders. But Ky citizens do not think like World citizens; they do not even think like each other. Their ideals differ as drastically as their tastes and talents.

"I'm better than the rest of you," one Ky businessman might honestly believe, "so my building ought to be the tallest." Another might bemoan: "I'd prefer to erect a modest ground-level structure, but my property is so small that I am forced to build ostentatiously high." Someone down the block from him reasons: "My business is risky and might fail; I'll build cheaply, small, and just for function." A banker next door tells his contractor: "Trim my bank with gold; shout my stability to the city." And next to the sparkling bank, a small grocer maintains the two-story rock-walled shop handed down from his pioneering great-grandfather.

Imagine any set of motives. Someone in Nyasport will have it. There is even, to this day, a single old rock church in the dead center of town—surrounded by technological marvels—where several hundred devout believers still perform prayer pottings, have their children's wings removed ceremonially, and cry penance for despoiling the natural beauties of Ky's all-but-lifeless desert plains.

Nyasport's only constant is change.

In 4108, three years prior to the point at which our narrative has arrived, a bankers' cooperative bought up an entire dilapidated section of northern Nyasport—except for one shabby rambling residence whose owner refused to sell at any price. The co-op first widened and repaved the old streets, thus attracting new buyers, renters, and customers. In the space of half a year, the look of the entire sector was altered. Skyscrapers rose as if yanked from the ground. Still the shabby home stood there, the undeveloped lot giving the new row of towers the look of a missing tooth. Did the bankers resent the obstinate family? Not really. On Ky, when land is owned, it is owned utterly, outright, and forever—until it is sold, given away, or abandoned. Did the wealthy neighbors and merchants feel sorry for the poor members of the household? Certainly not; the owner had let a fortune slip through his fingers. But to hide the eyesore, the co-op erected a wall around the property. Were the family members ashamed or insulted? Hardly; this measure of privacy within the big city had been their dream for a generation; and after the wall was up, they said so. Were the builders of the wall resentful for thus being used? No, they were amused, and pleased that everyone's purposes had been adequately served.

Behind that wall, where the tooth was missing in the skyline, dwelled an unsuccessful inventor with his wife and son, on that piece of land which had been the finest acquisition of his deceased prospector-father. The only gadget on which the inventor ever received royalties was a tire-gauge he devised in 4092; the money for this never stopped coming in, but it no more than filled the needs of his esoteric laboratory and workshop. The family lived off its garden and poultry coops.

As a public-relations gimmick, in 4105, the inventor renamed his family. He became Electron Stardazzler, and he called his wife Crystalline and his son Rocket. The ploy got him a tiny human-interest item in the local newspaper; then Ky re-forgot about him. The "great wall" incident of 4108 again got him the public's attention; but he proved unable to interest a soul in his current projects—even as he was being cheerily walled away from busy Nyasport.

Crystalline Stardazzler was still, though half her life was gone, an aspiring songwriter. She made the rounds of publishers almost daily. The publishers seemed to like her, even occasionally treated her to lunch, but they were unanimous in their dislike for her music. One publisher actually bought a song once, but he hadn't the nerve to publish it.

Rocket Stardazzler, an unexplainably brilliant teenager, was the only family member who regularly brought in money. He was a self-taught agronomist who produced the fattest melons and fruits anyone had ever seen—and sold them on street corners. He was also good looking, tall and tan with big innocent blue eyes, and bisexual; in a financial pinch, he sold himself.

Rocket might have been the first to win any sort of fame for the family, had it not been for the events of 10m 4111. That was when his father, Electron, gained entry to the history books in a plethora of parenthetical remarks.

Electron called it "The Thing" and he had worked diligently on it for many months. Not even his wife and son were let in on its identity. "The Thing," he would say simply, "is *it*." He had never made such a sweeping pronouncement before, so Crystalline and Rocket believed him implicitly. "Let me help," begged Rocket; and for three weeks thereafter, he neglected his garden to solder contacts on what looked to him like an elaborate timing device. Crystalline was given her part to do: from her trips into the city, she was to keep Electron posted on any news concerning the Ky rebellion. Had Forest made his request for a meeting? Had Firemaker replied? Had a time and place been set?

Electron was gone for two days. He returned with a very heavy crate which he had pulled on skids from somewhere north of Nyasport.

"They've set the time and place," Crystalline told him upon his return. "They're going to Eldry, of all weird places, and Forest is blasting off in ten days. There's a big special meeting of the Town Council called for day after tomorrow, at which the final plans will be discussed. Is that what you're trying to be ready for?"

"Yes, yes, yes, oh keeper of my heart," he said, biting her arm; "and I *am* going to make it!"

The next evening, around supper time, Electron Stardazzler danced into the kitchen, hugged his wife and son, and said, "I'll tell you all about it after I take a bath and shave."

"The Thing is finished?" Rocket asked excitedly.

"Yes, yes, yes," Electron intoned as he dropped a trail of clothes between the kitchen and the bathroom.

Crystalline and Rocket had a surprise waiting for him when he emerged naked and dripping and plopped into his favorite living-room chair. She was at the xylophone and her son was at her side. They sang:

155

What wonders does the genius bring,
Into the living room?
What's gonna make the chimes of money ring,
And all our laughing zoom?
At last fame and fortune are just outside
   our door.
What will they see inside?
Oh what, oh what is The Thing, my darling?
What, oh what, is The Thing?

Electron was blubbering tears of gratitude and exhaustion when he rose to squeeze them both. "Come along, come along to the lab, my darlings. I'll show you."

It looked like some portion of a rocket engine, or a very large complex steam-cooker. Cylindrical with conical caps at the ends and heavy bolts holding it together, it looked as if it weighed so much it could never be moved. A panel of dials and lights protruded from the upturned side.

"I'm not the author of the theories behind this," Electron confided, "nor even of the basic design. But I'm going to be remembered as the first man who ever built one. It's for the cause. With this, we can handle whatever World throws at us. This will make us invincible. I made it for Forest to take along with him; and it's finished, so he can."

"What—?" Rocket began impatiently.

"My loving son, The Thing is an atomic bomb."

Electron got precisely the reaction he expected: his wife and son were speechless.

Rocket slowly put out his hand and rested it on the cylinder. "It isn't hot," he said.

"Better not be," Electron said gleefully.

Crystalline said, "It's awesome, dear."

The three of them stood there in silence a while longer, staring at The Thing hardly blinking.

"I smell something burning," Rocket said. He moved in closer to check the exposed wiring at the panel.

Crystalline pulled him back. "I've burned the dinner," she explained, biting her lips.

"Good," said Rocket. "I'm taking us to a restaurant—to celebrate."

"But," she protested, "we don't have any money. Do you have any money?"

"Let me worry about that," said the handsome boy.

"It's a deal!" Electron said as he sprinted for the bedroom. "I can be ready in five seconds!"

CHAPTER THIRTY-THREE

Nyasport Mandates A Mission

Electron Stardazzler had never attended a meeting of the Ky Town Council—out of principle, he would tell you.

Even when his conflict arose with the bankers' co-op, he refused to appear at Council, as he was requested to do. He said, "There's nothing to discuss. Do what you will around my land, and nothing whatever on it." He then sat on his porch, under his sagging corrugated tin roof, smoking his favorite brand of weed, until they came to describe the sort of cage in which they proposed to put him. "Fine," he said; and this was his closest brush with the self-appointed guardians of Nyasport.

He considered those who bothered with politics effete and pretentious—people who hadn't the gumption to stick to their own goals nor the decency to leave everyone else to theirs. Meddlers. And on Ky—unlike World—such meddlers could be most often ignored.

Electron experienced some measure of confusion, therefore, when he awoke on meeting day, 4d-11m 4111, and found himself ecstatic over the prospect of laying his grave matter before the Council. His feeling was not, "I'll show them!" as he would have expected it to be; it was more on the order of, "At last I'm worthy to be one of them!" His emotion unseated his cynical attitude and left him with childlike anticipation.

The previous night, after their celebration supper, Electron and Crystalline had returned home (Rocket had stayed with the restaurant owner) to work for many hours copying, neatly and lovingly, the plans and specifications for The Thing. It was these, in a tight-wound roll, that he had under his arm when he struck out, whistling Crystalline's "The Thing," for the Town Council Hall. It was late morning; he believed he had ample time before the gavel came down at the start of evening.

He gently shoved a guinea hen aside with his foot, opened the door the bankers had been generous enough to provide in the wall, and stepped out onto a moving sidewalk busy with shoppers. The noise of clattering carts, the frequent shouts of greeting, the laughter of children chasing one another, the beeps of cycle horns (no automobiles were allowed in the co-op area), the hawking of peddlers—all these blending reminded him again how lucky he had been to finagle his wall.

He glided several blocks on the moving belt, alighted at a sidewalk tram terminal, and availed himself of the free ride for shoppers to the parking lot—which brought him to the interface with Valley Town, a sector operated by Nyastruth Real Estate.

"Have you business in our district, and if so, with whom?" asked a gate attendant of the red security service.

"Passing through," said Electron. "Thought I might stop for a bite to eat."

The attendant took his name and address and waved him in, saying, "If you use this route regularly, you'll be asked to buy monthly passes."

"I'd walk around first!" Electron said indignantly.

"Suit yourself," said the bored gateman.

Valley Town was in dire need of repair; perhaps this accounted for the discourteous gateman. The roads congested with automobiles were filled with potholes; the old brick sidewalks were too narrow and were rippled with wear; security police—from the three major services plus numerous local ones—were everywhere, owing to the area's growing reputation for pickpockets; while street-level stores and shops were in good shape, the several floors above them were largely in need of cleaning and painting.

With all the shortcomings of the area, however, this was the region where World visitors would feel most at home. It was quaint, artistic, old. And the odors in its streets were extraordinary; for this was the bakery and candy center for the city. A day's output here could feed most of Ayatsport for a week! (This area developed largely because of low street and maintenance fees charged by the developers, and the small parcels of land initially offered.)

At a sidewalk cafe, where he spent half the coins he carried on a fresh bun and hot tea, Electron heard a voice coming from a nearby radio: "... and all seats at the Town Council Hall have been reserved. Not since the decision to oust World representatives has there been such a...."

Electron jumped to his feet, spilling his drink, and ran.

"Hey, you forgot your papers!" the proprietor yelled.

Electron skidded to a halt, grabbed the roll of plans, said, inexplicably, "No, no, no!" and continued, zigzagging through the crowd, to the next border.

Here he encountered an unfamiliar white marble wall. Had he made a wrong turn, headed in the wrong direction? No—he had reached the rails of the Third-Circle train, beyond which stretched this new impasse— the top rim of which was a comb of stainless-steel spikes, to prevent trespassing. Electron followed the train rails for some distance—until he encountered a group of indigents, evidently hoping for handouts, near an open iron door.

The guards there were two in number and wearing green—obviously in exclusive employment. "I'm terribly sorry," one of them said to Electron, "there's absolutely no admittance with authorization."

"What is this place?"

"The Greenfield Estates—strictly residential."

"How can I get to the center of the city?"

"The shortest way around is to the east."

Electron shrugged—and ran.

He ran through a manufacturing district, through the Freedom Village low-income residences, onto the Second Circle Railroad (which took his last coin), to the transport docks where he hitched a ride with a trucker to the center of the city.

The Town Council Hall is, according to Ky reckoning, an ancient building; it is eighty-five years old. In it, decisions are made which can affect the lives of the citizens who built a city around it. But here the similarities to Parliament, the Palace, the Garden and the Glen cease.

The structure itself is nothing but a big rock slab with small clear-glass windows. Had it been erected on World, we might have assumed that once the decor was added, it would be a warehouse; if we assumed it complete, it would seem that some insufferable arrogance had surfaced in the architect, who wished to express pride in his own proportions rather than humility before the Gods. The building was made to resemble more a pot than a flower, more an egg than a creature, more a stone than a statue.

Ky's Town Council meets informally on the first of every month, or whenever a special need is felt. No one must, and anyone may, attend. Its decisions are never more than recommendations—with the likelihood that they will be accepted dependent upon the quality of the reasoning behind them. There is absolutely no enforcement, beyond popular support or boycott; but it should not be assumed that the Council's deliberations are taken lightly: for everyone at Ky knows that the Council is their only instrument for keeping Government at bay.

The Hall is owned and operated by the venerable Town Hall Committee—which is financed by the voluntary contributions of citizens who are prominent, or who like to have it thought that they are. Their contributions are posted on the outside door to the hall, as are ledger sheets showing the Committee's current fiscal state. Even during the decades of World rule, the Hall kept its reputation for operating with a surplus of funds.

There was a mob outside the Hall that day, and Electron Stardazzler pushed his way thoughtlessly through it to the main door. There was a large sign taped beside the contributors' list, which said: SEATING IS CLOSED FOR TODAY'S SESSION. There was also a list of the principle questions to be introduced; it included:

- How should remaining funds be raised to finance Forest Singer's mission to Eldry?
- Is Forest Singer entering a trap? If so, what means of protection could be provided him?

- Should alternate plans be considered, or should Forest Singer receive total support?
- Is Ky in danger of attack by World forces if Forest Singer should fail? Even if he suceeds?
- Does the merger of security services pose a threat to citizens of Nyasport?
- Is the effluent from the Winterwind Engraving plant a health hazard?
- Should the acquiescence denied the City Center Casino Corporation be reconsidered?
- Should piped water be encouraged to flow along the First and Second Circle Railroads?

Plus numerous additional domestic concerns.

A loudspeaker rigged outside the hall was carrying the proceedings—which were already underway:

"As I see it," a woman was saying, "financing is the only real question here. If there is money available for it, we have no business discouraging the mission. Yes, Canal Winetender?"

"Then the question comes down to: How many people and ships should we send with him; for that regulates the cost."

Electron slammed his fist against the door repeatedly. His answer came over the public address system: "Stop that banging! The Hall is full!"

Another amplified voice said, "Perhaps it's time for another announcement. Radio and picture-radio facilities have been set up all over town, courtesy of the Nyasport Broadcast Network. The largest of these overflow spots is the Infidel Theater. If the matter strikes one of vital concern, and it is addressed to one of the points listed on our posted schedule of questions, then one may participate from one of these extensions. Now, where were we? Forest, do you have a comment?"

Forest's voice said, "I'm going to Eldry, with or without your financial support—"

He was cut off by an outcry from many who evidently wished him to know he had their generous backing.

"And I am going with a small crew in an unarmed ship—"

This time the outcry was one of protest. Forest shouted

it down: "Because I don't want a repeat of the *Monz* disaster!"

A man shouted above the uproar: "The World bastards goaded us into that!"

Forest said, lightly but with emphasis: "I want associates at Eldry who are completely ungoadable."

Electron's panic was adulterated by a measure of incomprehension. Forest was going *unarmed*? That was preposterous! The people who love Forest Singer, and the spirit he represents to them, would never permit it—never, never, never!

That decision reached, pure panic returned to Electron Stardazzler. "Where's the Infidel Theater?" he demanded of a bystander.

"You're serious? You don't know?"

"I don't get around the city much."

"It's over by Greensman's canal. Just through Pioneer Town. Ask along the way; everybody—well, nearly everybody—knows where it is."

It was much darker outside when Electron arrived, his chest heaving and his legs throbbing, at the Infidel. He heard the loudspeakers from a block away; there was an enormous crowd here too. "I object," Forest was saying, "but I cannot stop you. I have to be honest with Firemaker and his party, though; I'll tell him our security services are sending additional ships."

"Tell him, by all means," said a woman's voice; "there would be no advantage in hiding the fact. But you don't really believe, do you, Forest, that they've sent their precious hero into space unescorted? I'll bet there's a military *fleet* following him!"

"If there is, he doesn't know about it. I've spoken with him since—"

Electron found himself facing another sign, this one on the opulent gold geometric patterns of the Infidel door: POSITIVELY NO ADMITTANCE THE THEATER IS FILLED.

A man at the Hall across town asked, and the loudspeakers at the Infidel relayed, "What sort of real danger is this alignment of planets? Is that all superstitious garbage, or—?"

Electron fell to his knees in despair, and this put his

nose against another posted message: ROOM AVAILABLE AT NYA'S TRUTH COLLEGE GYMNASIUM. He knew where the new college was—back in the co-op sector, not three blocks from his walled-in property.

He stopped at a public house along his route and slumped into a chair. "Nothing," he said to the waiter, "unless you can spare a glass of water." He rubbed his ankles, sipped the water, and watched the projected image from a radio-picture that wavered like a mirage on a white square painted on the green-plaster wall. It was the Town Council, where a kindly old man was speaking to a quiet audience:

"...certainly a paradox, but I'm convinced it was Unity that destroyed the World. Their only solution to war was to imprison the planet. Unify the people; unify their moralities, their philosophies, their psychologies and their expectations. Unify their productivity, their talents, their appetites, their esthetics and their tastes. The result was the homogenized World our forefathers found so intolerable they no longer feared prisons or death. But we must not lose sight of the fact that Unity has worked. They have no wars. Except for criminals and a miniscule band of individuals—like our Infidel and the man River—the people there *are* alike; and they're unified in their hatred of the free spirit of Ky. They must hate us—or face an overwhelming self-loathing for their cowardice. Good people, we delude ourselves if we hope the majority of World's population can accept our sovereignty. To further complicate matters, it's doubtful that the people under Parliament's thumb will even be told our intentions are peaceful. It seems to me that World's only hope, and in the long run, *our* only hope, is Infidel and others like him—perhaps generations of Infidels—who will press on relentlessly, to the death when necessary, for freedom of information on World. Only that can shave away at the congealed lump of stagnation created by Unity...."

When he arrived at the college, Electron's only urge was to lie down and sleep, right there on the mosses of the campus lawn. He heard amplified voices again, and his heart sank as he realized the Council had passed the subject of Forest's mission and were involved in another matter. Electron moved closer, leaned against a native birch, and listened.

Forest was saying, "...was in the nature of a gentleman's agreement, so we'll find nothing on paper, and the parties involved may deny it. But Ember Surveyor's daughter, Starlight, was present when the deal was concluded; she's here to tell you the specific terms of it."

"I'm not clear," said a man, "why you see so much danger in this. True, it makes the red service the largest; but some service or other is always going to be the largest. You say Protector is involved. I wouldn't be surprised, but his activities aren't illegal here. In fact I—and many of us—have profited quite a lot from dealing with him over the past years."

"My concern," said Forest, "is for the principle at work here. We say we have no government, that we are all totally free, that our way of life is invulnerable to political oppression as long as we keep the politicians and taxes away. But if a single individual or organization were to gain a monopoly of the security services, he—or it—could rule."

The hoot of disapproval was so vehement there was even laughter in it.

There was a sign on the gymnasium door too. This one said: PARTICIPANTS ONLY. ALL OTHERS CONGREGATE OUTSIDE.

"We'll take a question now from number nine at the Infidel Theater," said a voice. "We call on the representative of the Greenfield Estates' parents' guild—"

Electron tried the door. It moved. It opened.

Just inside there was a pretty young woman at a desk. She looked up at Electron as the door whispered shut behind him.

Electron was too fatigued to utter a syllable.

"You wish to participate?"

He nodded, his mouth hanging open, his eyelids drooping.

She took a form from a rack over her desk. "What is the nature of your business?"

"The nature? I—I—"

"The category—so we'll know how to number you according to the questions before the Council."

"Uh, Forest Singer's mission."

"You've missed that question, I'm afraid. The mission was approved."

Electron started to cry. He managed to say: "So important! It's about weapons, a defense for Forest."

The young woman looked around her, apparently concerned about inviting a disturbance. She rose and planted Electron in a chair opposite her. "Sir, I'm sure they will eventually return to your question, but I have no idea when—"

"It doesn't matter when. Sign me up!"

He took the numbered card she handed him, and wandered back outside where the night air was bracing. He was wondering how he could stay awake until his number was called. They were just now asking for number ten; his number was three hundred eighteen.

"Father?" called a shadowy shape running toward him. It was Rocket.

Electron somehow managed a very warm smile.

"I *thought* I saw you go in," the boy said. "What are you doing here?"

Electron shrugged, and Rocket understood.

"Are you hungry? I can run home and get you a sandwich."

Electron nodded. He showed his son the number he had drawn.

Rocket laughed. "I have a better idea. You go home and eat and get some sleep. I'll stay here and when your number comes close, I'll run get you."

CHAPTER THIRTY-FOUR

Annihilation With A Three-Year Guarantee

At almost the same time the next evening, Rocket burst in exclaiming, "They're up to three hundred and twelve! Where is everybody?"

He found his parents in bed together, snuggled close, speaking softly. Electron raised a hand to let Rocket know he had heard and would be ready soon.

It was a revitalized Electron Stardazzler who stepped to the gymnasium platform and spoke with good-natured confidence. "The one thing World understands—it isn't pain and it isn't prison—it's a threat. They're used to fear. Tell them they mustn't do this and they mustn't do that, and they'll believe you if you scare them. If Forest takes what I have for him, he won't have to worry about bodyguards or even guns. I made an atomic bomb for him to take."

Insignificant Electron Stardazzler had struck the city dumb. There wasn't a sound following his announcement, until a woman—there was no way to know which hall she spoke from—said, "Someone finally did it; he could blow up Nyasport!" Then there was some scattered laughter of disbelief.

"I'm serious," Electron insisted. "It's made. Ready to go. I've got proof here." He unrolled the sweat-wrinkled pages of his carefully prepared plans.

Forest Singer's image was five meters tall on a screen; his voice echoed in the gymnasium as he said, "Are those your plans? Hold them in front of the camera. Let's see the trigger mechanism... okay, now the shielding configuration... how about the reaction chamber and the two masses...there, where you have those black boxes—is that the explosive material for the detonator?"

"That's right. You know a lot about this, don't you; you ever build one?"

"No, but I've always been afraid somebody would. Do you have the chemical composition of the detonator?"

"Here—"

Forest said, "I hope other chemists are studying this. It looks too volatile, and at the same time looks as if the explosive would deteriorate."

Electron said, "It won't blow up by accident—unless you drop it into a sun or something; and the chemicals ought to keep their integrity for about three years, I figure."

"Are you proposing I take this thing along with me?" the five-meter picture of Forest asked the inventor.

Electron laughed. "That's what I call it, too, The Thing. Sure, it's yours; no strings and at no cost. I'm donating it."

"Where is the bomb now?"

"Safe. I guarantee that."

Forest was silent for a moment, deliberating. Then he said cautiously, "I'll accept your gift."

The gymnasium and the airwaves were so quiet it was as if Forest and Electron were alone in the city.

Beaming, the inventor said, "I'll hire a truck and bring it to the launch site personally. When do you want it by?"

"Lift-off is eight days away, but I'd like it as soon as possible. It will require some...special handling."

"I'll bring it tomorrow."

"I'd like to have those plans, too, if you don't mind."

"Sure."

Electron was as surprised as the rest of the planet's watchers when Forest next said, "Bumper—bring the limo to Council Hall immediately. I'll meet you on the roof." Then he vanished from view.

Another long silence was broken when the Council's acting chairman appeared in the picture and said, tentatively, "I think we should postpone discussion on this until our minds are fresher, after the dinner hour. May we have participant number three nineteen

...at...the Longshoreman's Auditorium?"

Electron found his son waiting for him outside.

"You were wonderful!" Rocket said. "They're talking about you all over town!"

Electron chuckled. "I was scared to death. You could hear what I said?"

"Every word."

"Where's your mother?"

"She got worried about something while you were talking and ran back to the house. Probably left something cooking again."

The port in the wall was off its hinges, propped aslant. Every light in the house was burning, and Crystalline sat on the porch chair, her head in her hands.

"They took it!" she sobbed. "They came and took the bomb!"

Electron and Rocket were too stunned to ask follow-up questions. She continued: "The red police, thirty or more of them! They just burst open the port and marched in. And they took it!"

"Did they hurt you?" Electron asked, white faced.

"No, they were polite. They even left some money for damages. They had to break a hole in the lab; the window wasn't big enough." The tears came again, and she babbled, "Not five minutes ago! Came and took it! They stole your bomb!"

CHAPTER THIRTY-FIVE

Weightless Cargo

The Marches of Man—a chain of tall rocky peaks to the southwest of Nyasport—serves the city as a shield. Behind the range are located many of the noisier and dirtier industrial facilities—Nyasport's atomic-electric plant (serving mainly industrial customers; most citizens operate their own, or community, generators), rail freight yards, manufactories, refineries, and the air and space port operated by Ky Interplanetary Transport. Honoring a favored astronaut, the port was once dubbed Fishbreeder's Jumping Off Place; now it's called The Jump.

The Jump had not rumbled and roared since the departure of a ship carrying Protector's "contraband" some months previously. Now once again, on 12d-11m 4111, the port was teeming with activity as ships were prepared for launch; and the citizens of Nyasport and environs gathered with their emanations of happiness, hope, and anxiety, to watch the awesome machines lift into the purple sky.

"Chaos," we feel obliged to state, is not an adequate concept to substitute for "anarchy," and Ky is done an injustice by the substitution; but on this day, "chaos" would certainly seem to have applied. Ky has no parade tradition to match Ayatsport's. If a parade is invited for an event deemed unworthy of attention, no one comes. If an event transpires which great numbers consider significant, they come by the thousands to create their own sort of parade. On the occasion of Forest's departure for Eldry, the city's daily routine evaporated; and the roads, trails, and skyways to The Jump were clogged as if some momentous calamity had driven the city to evacuate.

On the highway, car-to-car peddlers sold balloons, banners, fireworks and food. On the train, wares were peddled up and down the aisles. The wealthy and privileged came by air, and were met by salesmen on the ground. Even those who spent half the day hiking across the desert encountered those profiting from the event. There was conversation, argument, and laughter everywhere.

An Ayatsporter would have asked: Where is the pagentry, the beauty, the music, the dignity, the order, the tradition? A Nyasporter would have said: Don't you see them?

They celebrated not reverently but exuberantly, not as passive spectators but as participants, not as if they honored heroic achievements forever beyond their powers but as if each of them celebrated his own involvement in the happening.

But even on Ky the light of adoration can outshine three suns. As Forest Singer stepped from the shadows at the north end of the squat terminal building, he saw a valley of bouncing faces—many thousands of men, women, and children rushing toward him.

Their shouts and cheers coalesced into a weighty thing that settled on Forest's head, shoulders and cheerfully extended wings. He waved and graciously accepted the responsibility; but those close enough saw on his face a shallow smile. He was troubled.

In the distance behind Forest were four readied rockets poised on launch pads where numerous service cranes were slowly being trucked aside. The ships, built in different years, were of different designs; but they all bore the mark of the Ky mentality. There was nothing from nature about them. World's ships were whales; these were knives.

Forest led the crowd to the platform serving the moving walkway that would carry him and his crew to his ship—a ship his neighbors had built for him, a ship called *Arbiter*. On the platform he paused before an arrangement of microphones and awaited the arrival of six individuals who approached from the terminal: five adults and a little girl with wings.

The adults had evidently conferred on their speeches; for though predictable, there was little redundancy. The owner of the planet's largest chain of ore mines and founder of Goldtown, Manly Greenfield, said that only through cooperative commerce could true peace be maintained (his uranium and molybdenum mines depended upon World as a customer). Glen Brickman, who had been provincial mayor of Nyasport under World Government, recommended that Forest appeal to World's self-interest (and a woman shouted that the people of World had none). Ivy Warrior, a woman famous for her charities, praised both Forest and Firemaker and suggested that Forest invite Firemaker's entire team to come live at Ky, "where they're appreciated unconditionally." The president of Nyasport Protection Enterprises pledged that no harm would come to Forest's party, no matter what cost was exacted from the red and blue protectors; and the president of Ky Security promised that his men in black would do all in their power to forestall violence of any kind. The little girl with wings—Forest holding a microphone down to her level—said:

"Just about all the lessons at Bridgemaker's School, lately, have been about World, our history, and your mission. The kids realized that the more the teachers tried to tell us there was nothing to worry about, the more worried we got. We think you're about to do business with a planet of crazy people—millions of people who believe that the suns and planets have brains and that people don't...."

The throngs started listening with indulgent amusement—then fell silent as they considered the bright child's words.

"...and all they want is for us to be like them so they won't have to be afraid of us. We have decided you are heading into a trap. What can they want to talk about? The teachers thought we were all wet at first, but then they started saying maybe we were a little bit right. The kids all asked me to come here and ask you not to go. We don't want to lose you. We figure the talks can be done over the radio."

Forest knelt to speak directly into the girl's eyes, and he saw that she was silently crying. "Bridgemaker's School is full of very smart kids," he said to her, smiling. "But don't argue with your teachers; at least, don't slow them down. Let them tell you all there is to tell about World and its philosophy. Get them to tell you about their science, their Age of Awakening, their art. Learn the best about them. And talk about the unpleasant things, the military things—about how expensive and difficult it would be for them to wage a real war against us . . . all the reasons why they really wouldn't want to do it. Ask your teachers how hard would it be to carry on a peace conference by radio. In fact, try that in class: pretend one group of you is here and another is on World; and try to have a débate among the time lags.

"Make sure they tell you all the things Isle Firemaker has done for Ky. He's their leader, you know, my grandfather; and I trust him completely. What I have to do is help Firemaker and Sky Tinsmith and the others of the World team to find the words to assure Parliament that mutual respect can be aimed for. We don't have to solve everything; all we're after is a beginning."

"Why don't they send somebody else?" she asked.

He answered as if unaware there was a desert full of people watching and listening. "I don't want to go. I don't want to give up two years of my life for this. I don't want to leave my business interests in the hands of others." He grinned. "And I don't want to miss the Athletic Exposition. But it's in the name of all these things—my time, my possessions, my loves—that I have to be the one to go to Eldry. If you found that you were in the peculiar position of being the one person most likely to secure a peaceful future for Ky—would you hesitate to do it?"

"No," she said with certainty.

He smiled and spread his hands.

She responded as children respond best; she bit her lower lip and threw her arms around her hero's neck.

The multitude responded as multitudes respond best—

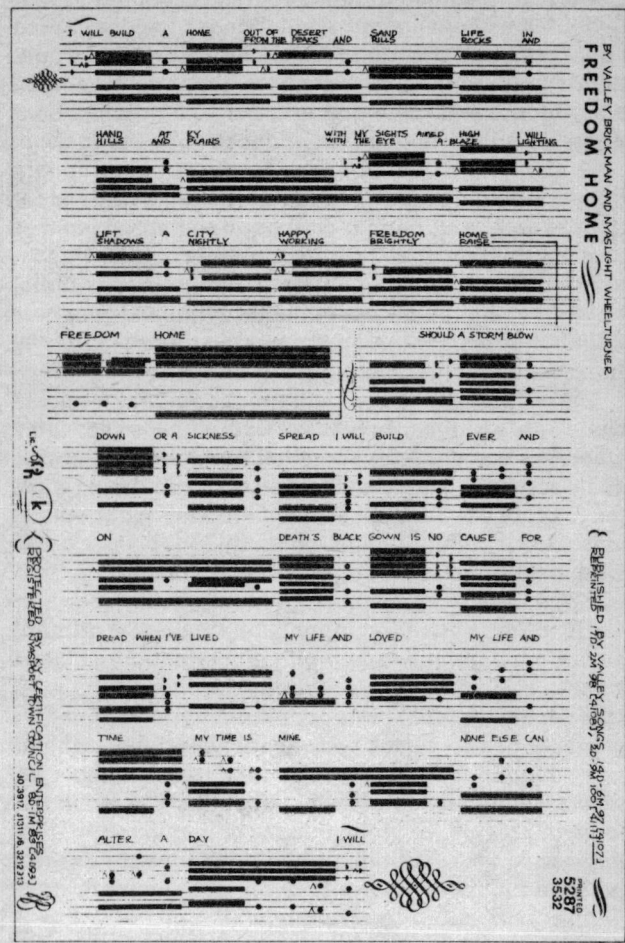

with cheers for the self-possessed little girl and for the generous winged man.

Forest lightly caressed her wing elbow. "Tell the kids I'll do my best."

She left without another word. Forest turned, gathered up his gear, and stepped toward the conveyor that would shuttle him to his waiting ship. The woman whom most knew or assumed to be Starlight Surveyor stepped onto the belt with him and rode out clutching his arm.

"Am I right?" he asked her.

"Father agrees with you. From what his investigators were able to find, he thinks the bomb is aboard one of your ships. He has no idea which one."

They kissed. To those watching from a great distance, it seemed that her return belt and his elevator to the silver ship's high hatch were agencies pulling them painfully apart.

Forest was aware of the fireworks bursting over the plains and mountain slopes, and of the cheers that came on breezes from all directions. He heard, filtering through it all occasionally, hundreds of voices singing an old work song that, on Ky, served as a hymn:

> "Freedom Home"
>
> I will build a home
> Out of desert sand,
> Life in hand
> At Ky.
>
> With my sights aimed high
> I will lift a city,
> Happy
> Freedom
> Home.
>
> Should a storm blow down
> Or a sickness spread,
> I will build
> Ever and on.
>
> Death's bright gown

> Is no cause for dread,
> When I've lived my life
> And loved my life
> And time;
> My time is mine;
> None else can alter a day!
>
> I will build a home
> From the peaks and rills,
> Rocks and hills
> And plains.
>
> With the Eye ablaze
> Lighting shadows nightly,
> Working
> Brightly
> Raise:
> Freedom Home.

When the sky was dusky with rocket exhausts, Monz flared blinding white twice in succession. World theologists would have debated long over whether this was an omen for good or for ill; on Ky the phenomenon was scarcely noticed and, by most, soon forgotten.

CHAPTER THIRTY-SIX

In The Vortex

1d-12m 4111: A lone black balloon slipped through low clouds over Ayatsport during early morning hours. Its loudspeaker claimed that Firemaker and his party were in good health and on course, that Forest Singer too was spaceborne on his way to an historic conference on mysterious Eldry, and that freedom was coming to World at last.

2d-12m 4111: In condemning the illegal announcement, the Ayatsport Press inadvertently confirmed its facts—except for the nonsensical freedom part. Since Unity, all the peoples of the World had been free, after all, free from war, hunger, disease, despotism, ignorance and unemployment. What other freedoms could there be?

But this minor event succeeded where earlier ones had not; it nudged the sleeping consciousness of World and said: Open your eyes; something unusual is happening. Requests for travel permits to Ayatsport increased, and in the capital city, people took to milling about in the streets for no apparent purpose other than to exchange information and opinions with their neighbors.

14d-14m 4111: Crime being on the increase, the boroughs of Ayatsport were subjected to a dragnet—north from the reservoir to the Spaceport in the south—in a search for more "chaotic disruptors." Hundreds were arrested, out of which only sixteen men and four women were sentenced.

2d-1m 4112: The Ky Athletic Exposition, held in

honor of Nyasport's centennial, was broadcast by radio and picture-radio throughout the inhabited regions of the Colony planet.

Two million kilometers away, Forest was bent over a receiver trying to tune in stray signals from home. The man sitting beside him—short, stout, with wide-set eyes and a faint perpetual smile—was his pilot, Bumper. They were bringing in only static.

"I can invent it for you," Bumper volunteered. "They'll say, 'And now the Exposition proudly brings you the incomparable flying team of Forest Singer'—and incomparable would not be an exaggeration—'which for a generation has symbolized mankind's lofty—'"

"...irect from...rt...adium...." said a faint voice out of the gray noise.

"That's it!" Forest yelled. He punched up the ship's intercom and announced, "We're getting something; I'll patch it through."

"...ribute to the...ity of Nyasport, the famous and exciting Miller Gymnasts from fast-growing Pottersville in the westernmost ore belt...."

The crew of *Arbiter* listened enrapt, peculiarly moved, as the stadium announcer described the feats of gymnasts, acrobats and exhibition athletes. Just as it seemed certain the flyers would be next, the signal faded away. It returned once more and allowed them to hear:

"...a serpentine, a spiral, a whirlwind of wings! Trailing colored vapors and lights...not yet joined by the young man called Wingmaster, who...poised...topmost...ower...." For a moment there was only static, then the voices emerged more strongly. "...icrophone at the summit. Meet the incomparable Wingmaster!" Applause sounded so much like static that it seemed the signal had died again; then came the voice of the flyer: "This is for my teacher, my leader, my best friend, the greatest man alive—for Forest Singer."

Cheers turned into cries of alarm; and Forest easily pictured Wingmaster's wing-straining rock-like plunge from the tower. The announcer was as spellbound as the spectators; he said nothing until the crowd had gone wild with approval. "The most incredible dive in the history of flight!" he opined. "Wingmaster is now flying at superhuman speed around the stands, just over the heads of the spectators...arms lifted up toward...entire team carrying streamers...lights...ther spiral...making a canopy over the stadiu...the Eye's light filtered through rainbow clouds which grow with ea...."

There was a surge of static, and the broadcast was lost.

Half an hour later, Bumper succeeded in relocating the signal, but only one clear word came through: "...Eldry."

1d-1m 4112: The Cathedral of Ayat issued one of its periodical Priests' Papers. This one excommunicated Sky Tinsmith and condemned Parliament for permitting his escape; and it chastised Isle Firemaker for allowing "Infidel" to board his rocket. It further stated:

"This ill-conceived conference at Eldry is an affront to the Gods and is doomed to failure. Monz admonished: 'Seek no exchange among pagans and infidels; bring them foremost before the Light of Ayat, whereunder thoughts can be read and understanding achieved (A3:8:3).' And Nya, through the prophet Wheelturner, said, 'An enemy of the Gods is an enemy of the people is an enemy of the Gods (N9:18:127).' And Syrdo admonished, 'And the true address of Freedom is Paradise, wherein the joyous Gods will reward the Custodians of the Garden with Love and Pleasure evermore (2S13:2:7).'

"Bring back Isle Firemaker while he still wears a hero's garland. Bring back Sky Tinsmith that he might suffer the ignominious burial he has earned by his blasphemous labors. Or the whole World will suffer."

Somewhat in contradiction to this dictum, a further paragraph predicted that the conference would never transpire. Conclave, the alignment of planets, would surely "swat down the human interlopers like gnats at a Royal supper," before they could even alight on the centralmost planet of the two suns.

1d-2m 4112: Parliament issued a secular paper which, for the first time in recent history, was not in accord with Cathedral opinion. "Before violence is resorted to, before we accept animosity as the norm in our dealing with Ky Colony, Parliament believes peaceful dialog must be attempted. Consider the heroism of Isle Firemaker: he risks even the displeasure of the Gods in his quest to save our lives."

12d-2m 4112: Parliament and the Cathedral were somewhat reconciled by Parliament's statement that "the Cathedral blames a rise in greed for the rise in crime; we therefore are endeavoring to draft a fair law which will evermore abolish both private ownership and the monetary system."

In the collonade outside the Glen, President Lightman uttered a statement in private which was overheard by a reporter from the Press. By some oversight, the statement appeared in print. The President reportedly said, "Ky has abolished all public property, and we've proposed abolishing all private. What do you suppose Firemaker and Forest will find in the way of common ground?"

5d-3m 4112: Firemaker's ship reached the midpoint of its journey.

According to gravitational theory, the farther a traveler moves from a planet, the fainter its influence. Psychologically, the reverse often obtains. Even a seasoned spaceman can feel, superstitiously, that his path has become an elastic cord urging him, with increasing tension, to return home. Approaching midpoint, there is often a fear that the cord will snap, and the traveler be forever lost.

"We have crossed midpoint," Firemaker reported to his ship, "and are precisely on course. The Gods be praised; all is well." He lifted his finger from the intercom switch.

"Is it true? Is all well?" asked Leaf Potter. She was visiting, strapped into the co-pilot's berth.

Firemaker switched the intercom back on and selectively eavesdropped at the various compartments. Just below, Friend Warrior and Sagacious Harvester were obviously intoxicated. Friend was drawling the verse to "The Flying Pig," and Sagacious was trying to interrupt: "Stop that! Must you sing that smutty... why do you do that?" Friend stopped long enough to reply: "To irritate you, I guess. Come on, Sagacious, sing it with me; 'Mother Pig shed a tear—' Come on, sing! Be carefree!"

The next compartment down, Sky and Merry's, was silent. Below that, two of the crewmen were unnecessarily calling off data on a check list, while the third—Firemaker guessed it was the cadet making his first space flight—whined unanswerable questions about dwindling food supplies, the likelihood of air leaks, the number of ships lost in the history of space travel, the reliability of this ship's pilots and crew, and so on.

Sky's voice came from a storage room below: "You really aren't frightened, are you?"

Merry answered him: "I'm not afraid the Gods despise me for enjoying myself."

Firemaker switched off the intercom once more. He said to Leaf Potter, "I had a crewman once who had the bad judgement to look out a viewport just prior to midpoint. All he saw was an unmoving infinity of stars. A stroke of terror killed him on the spot. Yes, comparatively, our people are holding up well." He asked, "How are you bearing up?"

"Passably," said the woman, "as long as I expend my worry quotient on others." She leaned across Isle Firemaker and switched the intercom back on. "You know," she said, "I'm growing fond of Sky—in spite of myself."

There are precious few secrets on a space ship. The two in the pilot's compartment knew that Sky and Merry had built a niche of privacy for themselves in the lower storage area, that they were probably lying naked in a hammock, their limbs entangled, as they spoke softly:

Merry: "What can I give you, Sky; my strength? My mind?"

Sky: "Your confidence."

Merry: "It's yours."

Sky (laughing): "That's ridiculous."

Firemaker reached for the intercom; Leaf Potter's hand stopped him.

Merry: "Is it? Are you becoming more, or less, confused when we make love?"

Sky: "Less."

Merry: "You see."

Sky: "But that's because my brain stops when my body is joined to yours. There is no longer a World, no crisis, no light, no darkness. There is less confusion because I no longer own a body, and there is nothing left in me that can think."

Merry: "You see; I have given you my confidence."

Sky: "And I have given you my soul."

Merry: "I'd call that a fair exchange."

Sky: "No wonder priests have not been permitted to love like this!"

Merry: "You're not a priest, my special love, and you never have been. The Gods, to you, are no more than ideas carried to theatrical extremes. Isn't that true? Isn't it? Do you know why you became a priest? To escape from the silly people that clutter the World—to see them only in Cathedral, where they sit immobile, empty, unreal. And they listen only to you; your voice, your truth, your guidance. Isn't that true?"

Sky: "No."

Merry: "Are you certain?"

Sky: "I—I don't know."

Firemaker insistently silenced the intercom; and he and Leaf Potter sat together for a long time without speaking.

10d-3m 4112: Forest Singer's ship reached its midpoint; and, in accordance with Colonial merchant-ship tradition, the crew celebrated with a Fear Festival.

"When I was a kid," said one of the crewman to the others piled into the cockpit, "I was afraid of the dark. Have any of you fellows looked outside lately?"

"It's not dark out the starboard side," said another. "Nya and Monz are straight out, and Ayat's aft, unless we've rotated again. I used to be afraid of meteors. Deathly afraid, all the time. Then on one trip I started to think about how many planets and suns we've got that just run around sucking up debris like a vacuum cleaner—"

"They *are* vacuum cleaners... get it?"

"Ever imagine there might be living things out there in space, great huge space-ship-eating monsters—black like clouds, undetectable, indestructible—?"

Forest laughed. "Now that's a new one on me. Want to know what always scares me the most? The thought that we'd be all the way out here before we discovered we'd left something behind that our lives depend on—like a screwdriver."

"Did we?"

"See what I mean? Not that I know of."

Bumper returned from the toilet and saw that there was no room for him in the cockpit. From the hatch, he asked, "Has anyone here ever been to Eldry?" No one answered him. "Now *that* worries me a little."

Forest said, "There's an old base waiting for us there, a base that has survived for many years and is still sending out a beacon and scientific data. If sensitive instruments can survive the place, surely people can." He glanced at the chronometer flashing numerals on the panel before him. "Coming up on midpoint."

"The radio's on," said a crewman.

They counted the descending numbers: "six...five...four...three...two...."

A circus march burst forth from the radio; an announcer quickly cut in: "And there you are in the middle of nowhere! But you're *exactly* where you ought to be. Telemetry here places you on schedule and running smoothly. You're eleven point twenty-two minutes away, so we won't try any two-way conversations. This is your friendly fear-dispeller, Birch Butcher, incidentally, coming to you live from the studios of Station Nine in Nyasport—where we have a wonderful line-up of celebrities for you!"

The "celebrities" were friends and relatives with news of home. Forest having no family, the morale committee had thoughtfully chosen Wingmaster and Starlight Surveyor to be his well-wishers.

16d-8m 4112: Parliament cast its first three votes on issues relating to the abolition of private ownership—of land, material objects, and money. No pluralities were reached; and the Central Committee retired to executive session to reformulate the questions.

1d-9m 4112: Without authorization, the Ayatsport Press conducted a public-opinion poll. It showed that the majority of on-the-street respondents favored retention of private rights. "That's what freedom is," one was quoted as saying. The Press deduced that the people felt "it is not an overindulgence in legitimate privilege that is causing the rise in lawlessness; it is simply an increase in the number of people who have no respect for the law plus a failure on the part of Ayatsport's keepers of the peace."

2d-9m 4112: The Cathedral issued a public notice in support of the Press poll. It demanded a new series of purges to ferret out chaotics, and an all-out effort to apprehend Protector and his pirates, whose activities encouraged disrespect for moral authority.

3d-9m 4112: Parliament reacted to the will of its voters and its spiritual head: it declared Ayatsport under martial law, imposed curfews, established each first and eighth days as all-city purges of chaotics, and tabled the volatile matter of rights until after Conclave. Protector's hideout—to everyone's amazement—was found (after a generation of mystery) and destroyed. The Ayatsport Press concluded its stirring account of the ambush on People's Island by saying that not only were there no pirates apprehended there, there was also evidence that everything of value had been removed from the hideout before the attack.

4d-9m 4112: The editor of Ayatsport Press was relieved of his position but was not otherwise punished.

10d-9m 4112: Balloons dropped epistles on Ayatsport, Stormsville, Irontown, Nxoport and Nya's Landing. The single sheet announced that the editor of Ayatsport Press and several of his faithful aides had defected to the underground anarchist movement—where they would devote their lives to the fight for freedom of information. The epistle was signed by the defectors in question over the flamboyant signature: River.

16d-10m 4112: Ember Surveyor, previous owner of Nyasport's blue security police, left his office at Ky Protection Enterprises and never returned. A red-guard team was dispatched to hunt him down, bring him before the Town Council, and have him branded dishonorable for breach of contract. His daughter, Starlight, told the news media that she had no idea where he was, but that, "you all know my father to be an honorable man. It's his contract with the monopoly service that ought to be ostracized."

4d-15m 4112: Forest had his final conversation with Ky prior to arrival at Eldry. He spoke to Starlight Surveyor; but he felt sure the rest of the planet was hearing him. Through the long eventless journey he had spent a thousand hours engaged in the kind of thought that distinguished him: he saw not men but events, then not events but trends which yielded to principles which gave way to ideas—which showed him futures.

The futures Forest saw were these:

Two planets respecting their differences, enjoying trade to mutual advantage. This, of course, was the hoped-for outcome of the coming conference; but there were many cultural obstacles in front of it. Unless public sentiment changed radically, quickly, Ky would continue to express contempt for a people content to exchange freedom for a perpetual childhood of automatically satisfied needs and a view of life glued together by a preposterous superstition; and World would forever despise a people kept happy by their life of irresponsibility and crime.

Two planets, forever strangers, awaiting the technological advances which would make war economically feasible. This had an advantage: Ky might profit from the challenge always to stay a scientific step ahead of the sluggishly progressing World.

Two planets progressing separately, in secret, with all contact, communication or commerce forbidden. This would be but a fleeting respite; for a thing forbidden is a thing perpetuated. Spying would become an obsessive pastime; war would be inevitable.

Two planets agreeing to live in peace, ostensibly under the dictates of World's Unity—with freedom but an unfathomable memory. A year ago, Forest would never have considered this a possibility. But now—if Protector established a renegade dictatorship at Nyasport, with an unlikely—but conceivable—alliance with World Government. . . .

To his credit, Forest did not—in his attempt to find solutions—begin with the assumptions that Ky society was perfect and only World society was flawed. On 4d-15m 4112 he said to his people:

"Somehow, the Town Council must raise the money to buy out Ky Protection Enterprises and any other major police services. Defense, at the Colony, ought to be run in the same manner as the Town Council Hall: voluntarily, without taxes, as a public institution. I know this idea will be abhorent to many, because it will sound like a proposition for government. But it is the only course I can find that might guarantee our freedoms."

Twenty minutes later Starlight Surveyor replied:

"It's too late. Ky Protection has now acquired the black service. It is a monopoly, for all practical purposes."

Forest advised:

"Try it anyway. If the Council can come to understand my reasoning, and the monopoly refuses to sell even at a generous price, then we can know they mean to attempt to subjugate us."

2d-18m 4112: With Eldry only a matter of days away, Forest and Firemaker located each other's vessels and made direct radio contact.

To Forest, his grandfather was more than the hero World and Ky thought him to be; he was also a friend. To Firemaker, his grandson was more than a beloved child who made him incomparably proud, he was the promise of a better tomorrow. Yet their conversation was businesslike, essentially impersonal:

"I have not come alone," Forest began. "Three other ships were prepared by Ky security services to escort and protect me. But I have their agreement to remain in orbit unless they're called upon for assistance."

Firemaker answered: "Something like that was to be expected. I, too, have an escort—a heavily armed one."

"We believe that aboard one of our ships—not mine, for we've searched—there is a crude atomic bomb. If such a claim is made by the captain of any of our escorts, I suggest you take him seriously. I have seen the plans for the device, and I suspect it will function. I haven't the vaguest notion as to the magnitude of its power."

Firemaker laughed. "Forgive me, son, but that seems the least of our worries. How many are in your negotiating party?"

"Just myself, essentially. And I'm counting on you and Sky to, well, lean in my direction. All I hope for is assurance that Ky will not be invaded by World forces."

"That's all, is it? You'll be facing four of us—each with differing and very complex ideas: Leaf Potter, representing Parliament's Central Committee; Friend Warrior, a staunch supporter of World's collective happiness and a pilot with political aspirations; and Sagacious Harvester and myself—both of us with some Ky sympathies, but both of us committed—genuinely committed—to protecting World's interests."

"Why haven't you mentioned Sky and Merry?"

"If they take any active part, it can only be as part of *your* team... if you think it's wise to associate your cause with two escaped traitors. Do you want them?"

"Of course! Please tell them I said so."

"They heard you."

"Firemaker—you're hesitating. What are you not telling me?

"Oh, I'm not telling you all the fears and suspicions I've stumbled upon over the past months—just as you're not telling me yours. And there's something... I suppose Sky should be the one to tell you."

"Put him on!"

"Forest? Can you hear me?"

"Yes—and what a pleasure that is, old friend!"

"Forest, it's about Merry and me...."

Forest listened to Sky's effusive catalog of Merry's virtues and felt that he had heard the list before, coming from his own head. The longer he listened, the more uneasy he felt.

The two ships were in frequent contact for the next several days.

10d-2m 4112: Both delegations, both shiploads of friends and adversaries, both armed forces attained equitorial orbit around Eldry.

CHAPTER THIRTY-SEVEN

Eldry

Ayat's Messenger is an oblate sphere of cometary ice, elements and salts which is equally at home circling Ayat or Nya, and periodically—as in the year 4112—traces for several revolutions a path that trades it back and forth between the influences of the two suns.

The planet spins at such a rate that it has no synchronous position; in accelerating outward to locate it, one would exceed escape velocity. It is as if the planet shuns visitors and perpetually endeavors to spin them off. Surface winds are fierce enough to insure uninhabitability—except in the vicinity of Syrdo's Wall, so named by explorers half a century ago because of its resemblance to a moral absolute.

The Wall is a protection, an omnipresence, and an overwhelming obstacle. It is a sheer cliff of white ice, twenty-thousand meters high at its center, and extending the length of nearly a quarter of the circumference of Eldry. If there were a corresponding feature in the opposite hemisphere, one would be tempted to see the planet as two halves joined slightly off-center.

With slight seasonal variations, the plain below the Wall is an atmospheric vault of relative calm—like the eye of a hurricane—which is bounded opposite the Wall by a region of tornadoes. The plain is warm, relative to the rest of the planet's surface, and the thermals it sends aloft shunt the falling drafts of icy air over to where the tornadoes form. Within that benevolent bubble, Eldry Base awaited.

"...and as the noble Messenger swings in toward the

heat of Nya," Firemaker explained to his team, "one might say Nya's feminine warmth, the subliming and evaporating and upward snowing of ions and ashes causes the planet to exude what amounts to an orange comet's tail."

"Eldry's Plume!" Friend Warrior realized aloud. "You mean all that lovely mythology is accounted for by nothing more miraculous than an excess of sulfur and sodium?"

"Perhaps," Sky ventured, "the Gods offered us these rather simple phenomena, these signs and symbols, that we might arrive at the mythology which would teach us the divine life."

"Hear hear!" said Leaf Potter nervously. Facts—such as those she now flirted with—did not blend with her lifelong beliefs.

"Nonsense," said Merry Weaver. "The planet came together out of whatever matter was available at its orbital distance from the suns. It requires nothing miraculous for it to behave according to its natural makeup; a miracle would be required to *prevent* its plume."

"Take your berths," Firemaker instructed them; "we leave orbit momentarily. Don't be alarmed if we have a bumpy ride down. Friend, would you care to land us?"

"Very much."

"Have you landed at Eldry before?"

"No, but I'm sure I can—"

"I'll talk you down." When the others had left the command compartment, he added quietly, "Landing here is difficult. We've lost several ships down there. Program the automatic burn for conventional atmosphere entry. That's it. We enter, as you see, heading east; but our low approach has to be from the north to the top rim of Syrdo's Wall."

The passengers were slammed forward as attitude rockets readied the ship for entry. Those watching Eldry through a port saw a gradual flattening of the planet's horizon and the sweep of a thin band of night which separated the muddy green side lighted by Nya from the brown side ambered by Ayat. It was like the sweep of a titanic instrument dial.

Just as sensors began registering the friction of the upper atmosphere, and while the sky was still black and clear, there was a quick white flare—like a salute or a warning—from far-traveling Monz.

"I hope," Firemaker muttered, "that the religious among us don't try to take that as an omen."

"Then—are you an atheist?"

"I suppose so, Friend. There's very little room for disembodied consciousness in the universe I have come to understand. Watch those heat sensors; they can give you an indication of wind direction."

"But you *can't* agree with Merry Weaver!"

Firemaker laughed. "I don't like agreeing with her; I cringe every time she makes a sensible statement. What do you think of her?"

"You're going to think I'm crazy, but she scares me."

"Me too. That's why I bought her scheme to put herself and Sky aboard. I had to know what she was after."

"And—?"

"Power. Over the Colony, I think; but I don't see quite how she'll manage it. Help me keep an eye on her once we're at Eldry Base. And watch those heat sensors!"

The atmosphere became as muddy above as below, and the ship bounced as if making a belly landing though there was no ground in sight. The air made a relentless howl.

Firemaker raised his voice over the shaking and the noise: "Now an arc over the pole to take us to base coordinates." He said into the intercom, "Turbulence should subside once we're heading south."

It did, and the dark orange surface of the planet appeared, drew closer, and zipped beneath at disorienting speed. It was a long journey, but every mind was in such a state of suspension that time slipped by as swiftly as the dizzying ground.

"Gods alive!" Friend shouted. "Dead ahead—it's Syrdo's Wall! We'll hit it!" He lunged for the controls to start a climb.

Firemaker grabbed his hands. "No—think! That's not the wall; it's a cloud over the edge of it. We're on top—approaching the drop-off. Flaps down! Hit the breakers! Enter the cloud slowly, but head directly into it. Once inside, we'll be right over the base. Descend immediately—staying as close to the cliff face as you dare, to avoid the tornadoes on the other side of the plain. That's it. Easy. Easy. They call the region of tornadoes Nxo's Wrath; the old mythical watchdog will tear anything apart with his spinning teeth—space ships included. Okay... now climb and lower your tail. Find the cliff face by radar."

They descended blindly, past where the ground had been, down—down more than nine kilometers through weightless mud—to emerge from the cloud still unable to see the base of the cliff. Rockets thrust downward, and landing lights converged in a point somewhere above the mist-enshrouded plain.

"There! There's the base, Friend; see it?"

"No. Oh, you mean that light spot? Where are the landing pads?"

"There are no pads; the volcanic plate under the ice will hold the ship anywhere. But see those little lines not far from the shelter? They're blast shields, to allow us to land near the building. Just line up on one and set us down."

The landing was steady; but when the engines had stopped, and all systems were idling, a rumbling vibration continued.

"Did I leave something on?" Friend asked.

Firemaker's face betrayed concern. "The ground is shaking," he said. "I don't know whether our landing set it off, or—"

"It's a quake?" Friend whispered, wide-eyed.

Firemaker shrugged. "Whatever it is, it's subsiding. Don't mention it to the others. Tell them to suit up and begin unloading supplies. You and I will go ahead and turn on the lights, heat, and air filtration."

Wrapped in thermal outerwear, their faces covered by masks containing particle filters and a short-range radio intercom, Isle Firemaker and Friend Warrior stepped onto the steamy surface of Eldry. The shaking had stopped—suggesting that the ship's landing had started it—but there was a pressure in the air, a roaring that seemed as steady as machinery.

Friend pointed to his ear questioningly, and Firemaker answered, "Tornadoes. You'll get used to the sound."

Friend looked southward and could see only a vague boiling black. In contrast, Syrdo's Wall—which loomed behind the black metal shelter they approached—was a sharply defined crystalline barrier rising perpendicular from the ground to the zenith where it dissolved into the gray of clouds several kilometers above. To the east and west, the expanse of ice was lined with irregularities, verticle crevices, but otherwise was the same: extending to a gray infinity just as it did above. But for the effects of gravity, one standing where Firemaker and Warrior were would not have been able to tell whether he looked into the sky or out toward a horizon.

On the surface, wisps of vapor snaked and spiraled over a layer of sodium "snow." Here and there steam escaped—as if faulty piping lay beneath; and where the yellow dust was thin, jagged maroon ducts—that must once have been rivulets of lava—could be seen beneath the ice. Eldry had breath and blood.

Friend noticed that Firemaker too was studying the ground. He had stopped and was running his hands through the dry ashen lint.

"What do you see?"

"Look back at the ship," Firemaker suggested. "See those lines emanating from our blast? Well, look here—"

Where Firemaker knelt there was a curious pattern of diamonds—as if blast lines from two sources had intersected.

Sky's voice came from their receivers: "What have you found?"

"Probably nothing," Firemaker answered him. He and Friend followed for a few paces the direction indicated by the strange blast lines. They shined out batterylights. No other ship could be seen in the dusky haze.

"We're ready to disembark," Sky reported.

"Come ahead," said Firemaker.

What the base's prefabricators had overlooked in the way of insulation, the dusts and ices of Eldry had accomplished. From just the heat of operating instruments, it was passably warm inside. Fifty-year-old light switches were quaint but operative; and once oil had been released into the heater it lighted quickly and burned dependably.

Firemaker checked his pocket watch and hastily switched on the massive antique radio. He tuned in his escort's frequency and reported: "We're down and safe."

"We read you," came the reply. "Our orbit takes us over your coordinates every forty-three point nineteen minutes. Coming up on center...hold...mark. Keep us informed."

"Where do you want these?" Merry asked as she entered carrying three cartons. The other team members followed her.

"In the galley," Firemaker instructed. "Sky, those are toilet items, aren't they? They go in the bunk area. We haven't started the heater in there yet; Friend and I will follow you. Sagacious, that's a recorder; it stays in here."

"I hope there's a broom," said Leaf Potter, "and plenty of soap."

"Check the galley compartments," Firemaker suggested.

There were no lamps in the hallway, and light from the main room diminished toward the bunk area. Sky nudged the door open with his foot and entered the dark room cautiously carrying his parcels.

"Here's a light switch," said Friend. There was a click, but no response from a bulb.

Firemaker snapped on his batterylight.

In the harsh beam stood six men with rifles casually aimed.

"Who are you?" Sky demanded as he set the cartons down.

They were dressed in unmatched thermals of green, brown and black; they looked more like mercenaries than representatives of any official authority. "We are the others," said one who was evidently their leader; he was tall, muscular, youthful. (Although Firemaker, Warrior and Tinsmith had never seen him, the reader would have recognized Honor Townsman.)

The perpetual roar outside took on the musical attributes of a bass chord as the dirty window of the bunk room began to glow from an approaching bright light.

"Forest's ship!" said Sky.

Their abductor smiled and shook his head. "No, that should be the flagship of the new Ky Consolidated Security Police—right on schedule. Shall we greet them?" he asked rhetorically.

CHAPTER THIRTY-EIGHT

Captured By Captives

Night fell suddenly, as during an eclipse, when the narrow band of darkness passed over like a sweep-second-hand and ended the period of brown light from Ayat. A few minutes later, Nya brought a dirty blue dawn to the windows of the shelter.

The outside door seemed to be exploded open by the perpetual thunder from the tornadoes, when five red-clad guardsmen hurried in, shivering. They wore no protective garments.

Townsman instinctively singled out the guardsman in charge and asked him peremptorily, "Did you bring transfer equipment? There's none here."

"Only a few skids and a manual hoist," the guardsman answered, gasping for breath. His eyes were on the floor. "Does Eldry always shake like this?"

"Apparently," Protector's man answered, unconcerned. "It will subside."

Firemaker said to everyone, and no one in particular: "Quakes are not normal here. The plate seems to be shifting, loosening, for some reason."

The red guardsman seemed for the first time to survey his situation, to note in sequence: the mercenaries with rifles, the stately man with white hair who sat casually in a foldable chair, the grim-faced middle-aged woman next to him; and the three who stood by a window—the one in pilot's green whose face looked ready to explode with anger, the small young man whose wide eyes expressed profound puzzlement, and the exquisitely lovely yellow-haired girl who stared at him in friendly amusement. He addressed the gray-haired man. "You're Isle Firemaker?"

"That's right."

"It's a great honor to meet you. I'm sorry it has to be—"

"Whose orders are you acting under?" Firemaker asked.

"Ky Consolidated Security," he answered proudly.

"Who's your chairman these days?"

"I—I don't know. It was to be Ember Surveyor, but he—"

Honor Townsman said, "That's enough."

Ex-Ambassador Harvester emerged from the galley with a pot of tea, a rack of cups, and an armed escort. He said to the guardsman, "I thought that was a familiar voice."

"How are you, Ambassador?" the guardsman asked, smiling.

Harvester introduced their captor in red. "This man's name is Field Orefinder. He was security captain at the embassy in Nyasport. He was the one, I seem to recall, that I trusted implicitly."

"You can still trust me, sir; you're in no danger here—none of you are."

Harvester shook his head. "The one I once thought intelligent."

Orefinder ignored the insult and addressed Sky Tinsmith. "Are you Infidel?"

Sky nodded, frowning.

"They're preparing festivals in honor of your arrival on Ky."

Sky muttered, "Festivals for their victims?"

Orefinder shrugged. "You'll soon come to understand what we're doing."

"When he understands," said Firemaker, "don't expect him to approve." He added, "In fact, I wonder whether you'll approve, Field Orefinder, when *you* come to understand."

"I know what I'm doing," he insisted.

"What?"

"We merely want—"

Honor Townsman cut him off, saying, "Keep your mouth shut! Harvester is right about your intelligence."

Firemaker laughed; he said to Honor Townsman, "You've just encountered Protector's greatest obstacle: the Ky mentality. Their way of life is so factual that they don't keep secrets very well. Orefinder was about to reveal something we already suspected—that I am to be transported to the Colony, treated as a celebrity, and held as a hostage for peace; that sanctuary is to be offered to Sky and Merry—who were to have been World's concession to you anyway, in exchange for Ky's reopening the World embassy at Nyasport."

Orefinder continued, confirming Firemaker's guesses, "And Harvester, Leaf Potter, and your pilot may either return to World in peace or come to Ky as honored guests."

Firemaker said to Honor Townsman: "You see—that's all he knows. Now why don't you tell him the true nature of his mission?"

Orefinder stared questioningly at Protector's man.

Out of the stillness rose a new thunder, another brightening light. The light dissolved into vibration. The shelter began to rattle. This time the floor buckled like an ocean wave; the walls cried out as metal tried to pull away from metal; dishes clattered and crashed in the galley; a stack of folded chairs tumbled.

"Conclave!" Leaf Potter screamed. "We'll die!"

Merry, standing at the window, raised her voice to say, "Forest's ship is down." She expressed no fear or concern; she was merely providing information.

Leaf Potter slipped from her chair to kneel on the rumbling floor. "Eldry doesn't want us here," she wailed. "Oh please intercede, great Ayat, and spare our lives!"

The rumble abruptly abated.

Field Orefinder looked down at the esteemed Parliamentarian and asked, sarcastically but with genuine curiosity, "Still believe in goblins, woman, at your age?"

She looked up at him with narrowed eyes. The insult, like cold water on the face, had calmed her.

Townsman said to the guardsmen in red, "You brought no thermal garments?" He seemed incredulous at their stupidity.

"They're in our ship," Orefinder answered; "we wanted to arrive—"

"Wearing your flashy red uniforms?" Townsman snorted.

Leaf Potter ventured: "Believe in superfluous symbols of power, young man, at the risk of freezing to death?"

Orefinder laughed. "That's a fair question," he said unexpectedly.

Honor Townsman signaled to his own men and addressed the red team: "Put on your thermals and get the loading over with. The sooner we leave this shaking comet, the better. Orefinder—go intercept Forest Singer. Brief him on the situation."

Friend Warrior asked Firemaker: "What loading?"

"I suppose," the hero speculated, "they didn't want to waste the trip and have brought contraband to be transferred to World. These mercenaries are Protector's men, you know."

Friend nodded.

It was a peculiar kidnapping, a cerebral event. Upon the departure of the men, Honor Townsman became the sole warden. He leaned casually against the galley counter—his weapon resting near him, ignored—as if he quietly enjoyed the peaceful circumstances, as if privately convinced that his charges were incapable of anything so undignified as an outburst of violence. The unarmed victims strolled at leisure, spoke freely, and eventually congregated at the windows of the west wall through the dusty frost of which they could watch men running empty-handed or trudging heavily laden over the smokey skin of Eldry.

Forest's ship loomed behind a nearby blast shield; it was the gleaming spire of a resting sword. Forest and Field Orefinder were silhouetted against the bright white of the concrete shield. Someone had brought Orefinder his thermal and mask; he gesticulated with whichever hand was free as he pulled on the suit. At one point, Forest grabbed Orefinder by the material of his jacket and seemed on the verge of striking him.

"Forest knew nothing about this," Sky muttered. "I've never seen him angry before."

Firemaker agreed. "Not even when he was a boy."

"I've seen him mad as a rabid bat," Merry said carelessly, her eyes never leaving the activity outside.

Forest's crew approached him and waited for instructions. He hesitated, shrugged, then apparently sent some of them to assist with the loading detail and others back to his ship.

The cynosure of Ky was standing alone, apparently absorbed in thought, when three men pushed a heavy crate into his view. He ran over to it. This occurred near enough to the shelter for the observers to hear Forest's angry shouts, but not the content of his words. The men abandoned their burden, left it lying there in the rusty snow.

Inside, Firemaker's sigh of relief attracted attention. So did his glance at his watch.

Merry addressed Honor Townsman as she walked toward him: "I demand the right to inform our people that we are being held against our will."

The outlaw looked at her curiously, unsure what to say.

Firemaker said, "She means, my friend, that unless a report is made to our escort ship within about—" he checked his watch again "—seven minutes, they will come down to render assistance. Then *your* ships will come down, and so on. I suggest you let her tell them all's well. We haven't the time, and I haven't the energy, for a shoot-out. Better still, I'll do it. Turn on the transmitter."

Merry Weaver and Honor Townsman looked into each other's eyes. It was Merry who made the decision and indicated assent by the faintest of nods. Townsman clicked on the radio.

The outer door opened. Forest Singer stood framed by it, reluctant to enter. Behind him, furry globs of orange snow were falling; and in places the particles floated or traced erratic spirals in the thick atmosphere. There was a crackling sound added to the constant thunder; it might have been from skids scraping over the rough ice, or it might have been from new electricity in the atmosphere.

After receiving confirmation of contact, the World hero said into the microphone: "Firemaker reporting. All is well here; continue to orbit."

"Right," came the reply. "We'll wait for your next report."

CHAPTER THIRTY-NINE

The End Of Eldry Base

Music emanates from faces—melodies which are detected not by ears but by souls that sum up symphonies in an instant. Forest looked into the faces of the captives; and the cacophony of their colliding songs darkened his spirit. His friend Sky sang of loyalty betrayed. The woman Forest once worshiped taunted him with the military tune that smacks of victory. The Ambassador he called a friend serenaded with disappointment, accusation, and fear. The pilot there, whom Forest assumed was Friend Warrior, played a sonata of treachery, of conniving. The old woman of World, her face rich with traditional instruments, sent him unresolved chords of curiosity, and a counter-melody of surprise—as if she had expected, once, to like him.

Then Forest's study found the face of his grandfather, and all that noise was conquered by quiet songs of affection, trust, sensibility, understanding. The effect was pastoral but not passive: a rhythm around Firemaker's eyes said there was quick work to be done.

Field Orefinder entered behind Forest, and closed the door.

Forest said to Honor Townsman: "You've done your part. Trust matters to me, and leave this planet as quickly as possible."

Townsman's eyes were on the bulge of Forest's back. The outlaw's expression said: it's true then—he has wings! Townsman asked, "What matters would you like entrusted to you?"

"May I have your rifle?"

"No."

Field Orefinder said, "Forest, we assume we have an ally in Isle Firemaker. Can you persuade him to come with us willingly?"

Firemaker shook his head. He said, "Ky is youth, and I am a four-thousand-year-old man who looks back to the cave of my birth—not with unadulterated pride, but with fondness. World's people and I love each other. I've not come here to sell them out. Nor have I come to help you import a dictator for Ky Colony."

"*That's* preposterous," said Orefinder. "We have no government for a dictator to seize!"

"Yes you have," Firemaker said, "and you are its representative."

"And who might this dictator be?" Orefinder pressed on. "You, Firemaker? Sky Tinsmith?" Then a realization fell neatly into the slot Firemaker had prepared for it; and Orefinder said: "Consolidated Security."

There was a high scream and a deafening crash. The shelter and its occupants were jolted like miniatures on a tabletop struck by a hammer. In one instant all was normal; in the next a gigantic cleaver of ice was imbedded in the ceiling and floor, and captors and captives alike were picking themselves up from where they had fallen.

The cause and source of the falling ice were clear enough.

One of Townsman's men threw open the door. "Listen," he said out of breath, "those crates aren't worth dying for. The men are scared to death and waiting in the ship to blast off."

Townsman nodded. "They have a point. Start the countdown."

Firemaker—being helped to his feet by his grandson—said to Townsman: "Has it occurred to you that once she's ensconced at Ky, she'll have no further need of Protector? Years will separate them, and her military power will guarantee her autonomy. Why should she retain her alliance with Protector? Out of gratitude?"

Sky Tinsmith stated a tentative fact. "You're not talking about Merry."

Firemaker replied gently. "There's only one thing a

despot needs more crucially than guns. A philosopher."

"He's crazy!" Merry insisted.

Pale, confused, Sky said, "But everyone on two planets knows *I* wouldn't support a dictatorship!"

Leaf Potter nodded abstractly. "To subjugate free people, a dictator needs to justify control as a protection for liberties. Sky, with you at her side, she could—"

Merry laughed. "That's the most fantastic notion I've ever heard! Don't listen to them, Sky!"

Merry's denial prompted only silence: the sound of reasoning.

Firemaker ran expressive hands through his white hair.

Honor Townsman spread his hands helplessly. "I've done what I was instructed to do. She's in your hands." He pulled open the outside door and held it. Beyond him, in the light of the external floodlamps, the weird snow was swirling upward.

Then Townsman surprised them all. He tossed his rifle to Forest saying, "Have a safe lift-off," and left, shutting the door behind him.

Forest Singer—peacemaker, arbiter, man of reason— and Field Orefinder—representative of coercion and conquest—faced each other, armed, frozen like toy soldiers. Their captives waited, impassive.

With Townsman's lift-off, the floor moved; a rumble— both felt and heard—increased. A faint glow from the distant departing ship appeared and faded against the eastern windows.

Orefinder stepped toward Forest Singer...and relinquished his rifle. "Arrest me if you must," he said.

"By what authority?" Forest asked with a shrug. "When we return," he added, "help me warn Nyasport."

Forest laid both rifles on the galley counter.

Bumper, Forest's pilot, pushed open the door. "We're counting down," he said.

"I'm coming," Forest said. "Prepare one of the extra berths, and program for the weight of an additional passenger."

"*Two* passengers," Sky implored.

"I'll not take Merry," Forest said.

"Nor will I," said Orefinder.

Merry said calmly, "Don't be absurd, Forest. I insist that you—"

Forest reached for a rifle and leveled it at her. "You'll return to World, old love, to stand trial for treason."

She walked audaciously toward him. He backed away until he was stopped by the counter.

"Take me to Ky," she implored. "Expose me; tell them whatever you will; ostracize me. I'll manage there. On World I have no chance—not because of this dictator nonsense but because I helped an enemy of the State escape. Forest—because I risked my life to save your friend!" She turned and begged for assistance. "Sky...?"

"Forest, please!" the philosopher cried.

"Stop right there, Merry," Forest warned, his voice rough and pinched.

She hesitated, only a meter or so from Forest, then took another step—extending her hands as if to beg, or conceivably to attempt to disarm him.

He fired.

The scream of agony came not from Merry Weaver—she perished before a breath could have stirred in her ruptured lungs—but from Sky Tinsmith.

Sky stood there, his gentle mouth hanging loose, his eyes vomiting tears; he moaned, gagged, as if something intended to be words tried to pass his throat.

"I'm sorry," Forest whispered to his friend, helplessly. He turned to Field Orefinder and said, "Get your men off this planet as fast as you can. We'll follow you."

The guardsman in red jerked his eyes from the mangled body at his feet—the body that, a few seconds earlier, had been distractingly beautiful—and nodded. Aware that time had not yet resumed its proper pace, he reached slowly for the door handle. Before he vanished into the cold cloud outside, his faint smile said to the flying man: thank you.

Sky—as if drawn to a vision in the fog that he alone saw—walked purposefully through the open portal and into the gray nothingness.

Forest dropped the rifle and called to him fearfully: "Come back, Sky; you'll get lost out there!"

To the others he said, "Grab your gear!"

With Isle Firemaker, Sagacious Harvester, Leaf Potter and Friend Warrior, Forest stepped out onto the radically changed surface of Eldry.

It was a forest of steam-trees which rose in jets and billows from the shattered plain. Visibility was to zero in places and to but a few meters elsewhere. Now and then a clearing in the columns floated by. The brown light from above was oddly brighter than before, suggesting that the mountainous cloud cap had thinned; and the strange orange ash was drifting upward. The tornadoes were ominously loud: the atmospheric changes had invited them to march to the ice of Syrdo's Wall.

"Did Sky have his face mask with him?" Forest asked, communicating through his radio intercom.

"I didn't see it in the shelter," Harvester answered.

"I think he had it around his neck," said Leaf Potter.

Sky's voice said, "Yes."

"Where are you?" Forest demanded.

"Don't come for me. I don't want to look at you."

"Then go to my ship. Now!"

There was no answer.

Bumper's voice came from the intercom. "What are you people waiting for? What's all this about Sky? What happened back there?

After a long wait, Forest replied, "I shot Merry Weaver."

"Speak louder; I couldn't hear that."

"I killed Merry Weaver."

It was then Sky's voice which asked: "Why?"

"Sky, you know the reasons," said Forest.

There was no response.

As the red flagship lifted off, there was vibration but no renewed subterranean movement. The rocket's rising light threw straying shortening shadows across the ground and over columns of vapor. Forest caught sight of a solitary white shape far to the south: Sky sitting on the ground.

As Forest was about to run toward his friend, Bumper bounded up to the group. "I've been listening," he explained. "I'll get Sky. You people board the ships—fast.

Both are on countdown minutes away from lift-off." The Ky pilot sprinted toward where Sky had been sighted; but by now that region was once more behind a wall of opaque air.

Forest turned to bid Firemaker goodbye—knowing that at Firemaker's age this could be the last time the two would face each other. Love and a lifetime had to be expressed; yet no words came.

Firemaker extended his arms and enveloped his cherished grandson. They held each other, barely hearing Bumper's calls to Sky—and the erratic breathing, the sobs, of the betrayed Infidel. But they heard Friend Warrior when he said:

"No. Forest is coming with us."

Forest looked into the barrel of the rifle which had killed Merry Weaver. Friend was aiming at his head. In the confusion, no one had seen him take it from the shelter.

"No!" cried Firemaker.

"Yes," Leaf Potter said simply.

"Gods forgive us," Harvester moaned; "but it is a road to peace—temporarily."

Forest addressed his intercom: "Are you listening aboard *Arbiter*?"

"Of course we're listening," said a crewman. "Are they serious?"

"A rifle aimed at me says they are."

"What do you want us to do?"

Friend snapped at Forest: "None of that! Shut off your intercom."

Firemaker commanded, "No, let him talk."

Forest answered the crewman's question. "Get Sky and Bumper aboard and leave without me."

Bumper's voice interrupted: "I see you, Sky. Come back with me, please! Haven't you heard what's happening? We'll need you!"

The *Arbiter* crewman said: "Time's up, Bumper!"

"Listen to me!" Forest insisted. By this time the group was hurrying across the plain toward Firemaker's ship. "Any attacks or missions of vengeance could obliterate whatever good my capture might do. You *must* do as I suggest. Are you listening, Bumper?"

"Yes, Forest."

"Wait until all escorts are irreversibly bound for their home planets before reporting this development. Then tell Ky I have surrendered by choice."

"But you haven't!" said the *Arbiter* crewman.

"This is the only way I can undo the treachery perpetrated by Ky's self-serving dictatorial police. Please report those exact words from me."

"But Forest, they'll kill you!"

"I know."

Leaf Potter said, as they ascended the outside conveyor toward the World ship's hatch, "Forest will have a fair trial. I promise to testify on his behalf."

Bumper said, obviously running as he spoke, "Sky refused to budge, Forest. I'm sorry. Terribly sorry."

Aboard World's ship, waiting for the instant when engines would automatically erupt, Forest and Sky exchanged their last words by intercom.

Sky: "But you loved her, too."

Forest: "I loved the woman I thought she was."

Sky: "Anarchy...is that what it means to you...the freedom to kill, to destroy?"

Forest: "That's what it meant to her, Sky. Not what it means to me—or to you."

Sky: "I don't know what anything means anymore."

Firemaker said quietly, "I think her first declaration, as ruler of Ky Colony, would have been to prohibit human wings."

After a thoughtful silence, Sky said, "I loved you. All of you."

Forest answered: "I loved you, too."

The World ship's burn commenced. Its passengers listened, over the violent rumble of lift-off, to *Arbiter*'s long-range transmission to ships in orbit:

"Firemaker's ship is airborne," Bumper's voice said, "and *Arbiter* is on final countdown...."

World's ship was in the buffeting winds of the upper atmosphere of Eldry when they heard a second transmission from Bumper:

"...massive quake as we lifted off. The plain has

collapsed. We toppled, but we're finally beginning to level off, turning. The winds are growing stronger here to the south of the Wall, but I think we can—" There the transmission ended abruptly.

It seems probable that on the open plain of Eldry, Sky watched first the ascent of Firemaker's ship—which must have generated the quake—then the erratically climbing fireball of *Arbiter*. He must have seen the Ky ship lean and blast diagonally toward the tornadoes, where—after vanishing in clouds for a time—it reappeared, spinning, tumbling, sailing like a stick thrown through the air—leaving a winding coil of smoke and flame—until it slammed broadside into Syrdo's Wall. A burst of red fire. Falling ice. Falling debris. Then an atomic white light brighter than the light of any sun. Then the black of eternity.

Through viewers aft, Firemaker's people saw the blinding dot that made it appear that a star had landed at Eldry Base.

Another long-range transmission was picked up by Firemaker's receiver; this one from Field Orefinder, whose ship had attained orbit:

"Firemaker's party lifted off safely, apparently. Forest's ship...did not make it. He...I...the Stardazzler atomic device was to have been transported to World, into Protector's hands. It ended up...Forest...insisted, when he saw it on the ground outside the shelter, that it be reloaded onto his ship for return to Ky and dismantling. I agreed. It...*Arbiter* crashed somehow during lift-off and the bomb exploded. Forest, Sky Tinsmith, Bumper and the others have to be dead."

Forest switched off the radio and said to Firemaker, "Let's leave it that way."

His grandfather nodded grimly.

Leaf Potter said, her amazement increasing while she spoke, "The Gods have aligned themselves, and allied themselves with World—clearly, without a single ambiguity. The will of the Gods has been accomplished. The favored were rescued and the wrongdoers have suffered. Justice is served—precisely!" She added, shaking her head, "But somehow there is no joy in it—not in any of it."

CHAPTER FORTY

A Walk In The Garden

9d-9m 4114: Forest Singer walked slowly the breadth of the Garden of Gods.

Never in his life had Forest experienced such a richness of atmosphere. Daisies, poppies, red mosses, flowering shrubs and fruit trees, and delicate vines surpassing the spectrum provided new treats with each caprice of the fragrance-bearing breezes. Nowhere on Ky were grasses so voluptuous as those now beneath his bare feet—intensely green and cool and tangy from fresh mowing.

The sky was uncommonly clear over the World's capital. Ayat, near the zenith, bombarded the planet with warmth and restored the missing gold to the facade of the Palace of Parliament, making of it a benevolent shrine. Nya shone too, a few degrees off the horizon; and even she was too brilliant to be stared at—as Forest wanted to do: stare at her until she heard him and called him home.

His mind supplied Starlight Surveyor's last words (relayed to him by way of the anarchist River): "We were all relieved to hear Parliament's assurance that you would be treated respectfully. Their comments were broadcast over all the stations repeatedly. There's so much to tell you; but you're so far away! What could it matter to you that the Clockmaker sector has been subdivided and sold off, or that through a contract that strikes us as innovative, the Banker's co-op has agreed to restore the streets of Valley Town. Oh yes—the flying team has agreed to perform at a benefit to raise funds for the purchase of Consolidated Security by the Town Council.

Nobody feels really easy about this, but the purchase seems to be going ahead. I love you; but that's hardly original, millions do. There was a big argument at Council over whether to ostracize Electron Stardazzler for building that bomb. They finally agreed it was better to keep him where they could see him rather than to send him off to some hidden laboratory. So they took no action against him. I love you, Forest. I know you'll come back as soon as conditions are right among the planets."

As he passed Ayat's Tree he caught the eye of one of the guards posted there; the military man offered the Colonial a faint nod of support.

Forest Singer walked slowly the breadth of the Garden of Gods with his grandfather at his side.

From time to time Forest would rest his hand on Firemaker's shoulder, but they seldom talked. There were strains of music coming from somewhere distant, but Forest barely registered the fact; he had many things on his mind:

The fantastic parade that had met Firemaker's ship upon their landing...the stunned silence of the crowd when they first saw the winged man...the hatred, the verbal abuse, the ignorance hurled at him like stones. Then his likeness had appeared in the press; the penman chose to show Forest Singer standing before Parliament in the Glen—a proud figure, his wings lightly extended, surrounded by the glory of the naturalist art of a thousand years. To Forest the picture was a wonder; and in spite of his differing politics, it made him feel oddly a part of the history of his race. He was awed by such a display of civilization, respectful of the authority represented in the Glen. But the picture caused rioting in the streets.

"I am here," Leaf Potter told Parliament, "not as a judge and not as a Witness, but as a friend of this body of lawmakers *and* as a friend of the man on trial." Murmurs of disapproval echoed in the Glen. "I do not defend the Colonial iconoclasm or its anarchy, merely the intensions of Forest Singer—which were, in every instance, to establish good will between our peoples."

Forest Singer told Parliament, and as he strolled in the Garden he relived his testimony: "My mission was not solely my own; I had the almost unanimous support of the Nyasport Council—who challenged me to restore harmony and normalize trade."

But an astute Parliamentarian noted that "the Council sent only one ship; your security people sent three and an atomic bomb. We should be dealing with Ky's police, not its Council." And another said, "The Unified World cannot enact a treaty with an individual, only with a government. And there is none at Ky." Yet another, angry as he spoke, said, "This absurd flying man ignores the heinous acts of violence committed in Ayatsport and other cities—by his own supporters!" Forest tried to answer him: "Infidel wrote essays; River and others tried to take his thoughts to the people. Paper and black balloons may be illegal here, but they are quiet, orderly, and peaceful. This was our only effective support." Firemaker rose out of turn to say, "I agree with that." Leaf Potter stood and joined him, adding, "If the Colonials had perpetrated the criminal activity, they would not have denied it; they would have claimed it proudly—otherwise the violence serves no purpose—from *any* point of view!" Others in the staid assembly bounded to their feet and shouted opinions. The session had to be adjourned to restore order.

In the palm collonade outside the Glen, a man dripping with luxurious gems and costumed as a plump peacock, a man with narrow eyes, of middle age and height, with frequent smiles that contradicted a sadness in his face, said softly to Forest in passing: "Even after all you've cost me, I'd still feel inclined to rescue you—if such a move were reasonably within my power. Unfortunately it isn't."

Forest felt the back of his neck tingle. "Why?" he whispered. "Who are you?"

The man smiled again, shrugged, and moved along.

Forest and Firemaker ambled beneath an arbor matted with yellow blooms. "Remember that picture that appeared in the Press—the drawing of me standing in the Glen?" Forest asked. "Would you see that copies are sent to Ky in the diplomatic pouch? I'm rather proud of that."

"Of course," Firemaker promised. He kept his eyes on the path ahead.

"Has Sagacious decided to return?"

"He's decided not to. His wife—he doesn't want to leave her again."

"Why don't they send Leaf? She's a fine observer. I think they'd like her at Ky—eventually."

"She claims she's too old."

"Nonsense."

When they emerged from the arbor, they could see through to one of the streets bounding the Garden, where a solid green line of Police held back a crowd. There were crocuses fluttering high above the perimeter like the tops of legless watchtowers.

Forest recalled an event a month—it seemed like years—ago. While being examined by Parliament, he had been lodged in an arboreal tower of the Palace, in a small rock cell with but a single unglazed slit for a window. There, an hour or so before dawn, his mattress spoke to him.

"Singer?" said a voice beneath his head.

He scrambled to a sitting position and listened. The voice called to him again.

He found a small two-way lodged in the springs. "Yes?" he said to it.

"Will you speak for publication?"

"Whose publication?"

"My name is River."

"Ask me anything, anything at all." Forest examined the compact radio and recognized that it was of recent Ky manufacture—likely from the crates of contraband transferred at Eldry.

"Tell us why the peace conference failed."

Forest relived the experience for River, including as much detail as he could remember. Gray light was appearing on the sill by the time he finished.

"You have now made your first visit to our World. What do you see as our greatest obstacle to freedom?"

"World's idea that the universe has a purpose, and that the individual man doesn't."

"Our best ally?"

"Unhappiness."

"And our best hope?"

"Truth. You know, education is not compulsory at Ky; but our most remote farm families are better informed than your graduates. If this interview reaches the Colony, for instance, it will be broadcast to all who are interested—and that will include almost everybody."

"We hear a rumor that Parliament is considering lifting its censorship of Ayatsport Press. You've been at the Glen; can you confirm this?"

"It wasn't discussed in my presence, but I understand it is being considered—due to the riots, the public confusion, the work you and your people are doing, and repeated requests from the current editor of the Press. He needs everyone's support—their vocal, non-violent support."

"What is your attitude toward violence perpetrated in the name of freedom?"

Forest thought it out before answering. "Your World is run by a democratic dictatorship. Unity ended your wars and enslaved you all—by your own majority choice. You elect your officials on the basis of their promises to you. What must happen—and I see this as a long heartbreaking struggle—is that you must begin to elect a new variety of promise. And that means ideological change. As soon as enough of your people want freedom, they can elect it. Reason, persuasion, insight—these are needed, and violence is their antithesis."

At the close of the interview, Forest suggested: "When you've set this in type, why not offer it to the Press. It might give the editor something concrete to fight for, if they're interested in publishing it."

"I will. And may I ask you . . . would it jeopardize your situation if you smuggled this two-way into the Glen?"

Forest laughed. "Nothing could jeopardize my situation noticeably. I'll be glad to try. I doubt you'll get very clear reception; there's so much metal in there."

But on waves of static, a signal thereafter carried to the public its first full transcripts of meetings of Parliament, including the last of Forest's trial:

"The Congress of the Cathedral votes unanimously

that the atheist revolutionary be put to death," said their representative, a man dressed in spangling robes, with a righteous and kindly expression on his face. He held the newly potted pine that had guided that Congress in its deliberations.

"My own inclination," said the Committeeman from the South Borough (which includes the Cathedral), "is to vote for his acquittal and exile back to Ky." There was a shocked silence in response. "But my constituents would cut my throat. Their demonstrations have made it clear that a man with wings is an affront to civilization. I cast their vote—for execution."

"My people are divided," said the man from the North Borough. "On their behalf, I recommend that the victim be stripped of his wings, and sent home." (Many noted his use of the word victim rather than the word criminal.)

The man from the Port Sector said, "I recommend acquittal," without explanation.

The young Parliamentarian from Stormsville—she was dressed as a toad—followed his lead. "Acquittal," she said. Before sitting she added: "I always wondered how even barbarians could have killed Friend Inventor, not in ignorance of his genius but because of it. I'm beginning to understand."

Many turned toward her with sympathetic faces. They did not agree with her, necessarily; but they realized that her openness would put an end to her political career.

The Member of Parliament from Winterland spat out his denunciation of "infidels out to destroy decency and culture," and recommended torture leading to painful death. He was shouted down by a majority who thought him sanguinary.

Committeewoman Potter cast her vote: "Brand him a criminal; our law demands it. But send him home unharmed."

There were other votes for dis-winging, others for execution, and one other for acquittal: Isle Firemaker's.

On a glorious day, 9d-9m 4114, Forest Singer walked the breadth of the Garden of Gods, his grandfather at his side, with many things on his mind, toward his grave.

CHAPTER FORTY-ONE

Forest Singer

9d-9m 4114: The tradition and symbolism of four thousand years failed. Reality was dreamlike because so many things happened that could not happen.

The best-informed mob in Ayatsport history entered the Garden through cordons of helplessly outnumbered Palace Police—and no one was injured. The mob was vocal and angry; but they walked slowly. They were determined but seemed not to know why, purposeful with no object.

With the failing of ground patrols, the fleet of crocuses increased in number; but they held their places as if mesmerized. They made the air rumble but caused very few faces to turn fearfully skyward.

The age-old execution hymns were sung by Cathedral choirs, but this day the songs seemed ludicrously out of place. The ceremony is supposed to taunt with songs of good cheer, to deliver a message to the convict and the World: not even through a life of crime can you or anyone act against the purposes of the Gods and men; you serve us now in your appointment with oblivion. But the crowd was not joyful, and the convict was not ashamed.

"Gods alive!" said a bystander near the grave. "Look at his face. He's enjoying the music!"

Forest was enjoying not the words but the melodies of happiness and hope.

The convict was naked, to humiliate him; but he seemed comfortable in the knowledge that his body reflected inner qualities of which he was not embarrassed. Some observers remarked that he looked like a statue out of mythology. They called him Eldry.

Ordinarily the condemned die alone; but Forest had friends beside him, friends unafraid of charges of complicity. They were Firemaker, Potter, Harvester, Warrior, several Members of Parliament who had voted for leniency toward him, and a score of citizens Forest did not know. They circled him protectively. Their circle tightened when the mob approached, then spread out again when it was clear the mob wished to come no closer.

The religious content of the songs had always been acknowledged by respectful silence; this day a group toward the rear of the mob struck up a conflicting chorus of "The Flying Pig"—presumably because they sensed that nothing less would sufficiently insult and condemn the convict. And no one tried to stop them.

"The Flying Pig" and the continuing Cathedral hymns were joined by a counter-melody from the sky as a black balloon floated by singing through the rumble of crocuses:

> I will build a home
> Out of desert sand,
> Life in hand
> At Ky
>
> With my sights aimed high
> I will lift a city,
> Happy
> Freedom
> Home....

A few on the ground joined in and continued the strains of it after the balloon had passed.

It was a dissonate blending. Many people sensed that it reflected the state of their World.

To make the criminal less than human, less even than animal, to make him fertilizer in service to plants—such was the intention of the ceremony. But Forest was heard to ask:

"These saplings to be planted over me—what are they?"

"Ky Birches," said Friend Warrior.

"They grow taller and thicker here," said Sagacious Harvester, "in spite of the heavier gravity. We think it's because of the richer soil and more moist air."

"There's one full-grown," Leaf Potter said, pointing.

"It's beautiful," said Forest. "I approve."

Guards approached to force Forest to his knees, to start him crawling down the ramp into the open pit; but instead they allowed him to climb the mound of loose dirt, stretch out his wings full-span against the bright sky, and float down unaided, unprodded.

Garbled shouts of both outrage and inspiration momentarily drowned out the Cathedral Priests who had begun to chant the Retribution from Syrdo. One might imagine that somehow all the certainties, uncertainties, fears, faiths, and expectations of Ayatsport had been extracted from the people and stirred.

The mob formed the shape of a funnel and began the processional. Strange to tell, it was orderly. A later account in the Ayatsport Press suggested that it was in part the presence of Isle Firemaker—standing there at grave's edge, his immobility, his stateliness, his tears, which kept the crowd in check.

The first handful was not, as prescribed by law, cast by the High Priest. Pushing ahead of him, Firemaker dug lightly into the mound of dirt, and as he opened his hand over the grave, he said, "Please forgive me the role I had to play in this crime." It was not clear to observers whether he spoke to Forest, to the people, to the priests, or to the Gods.

Forest called up to him: "None of us did other than what we had to do—because of who we were, where we were, and what we thought ourselves capable of."

Many flung dirt spitefully; as many others reached the grave and ran, refusing to drop their handfuls.

Nya had set and Ayat was low when a youth dared to kneel at graveside. He was a stranger to Forest and the others standing near; but the reader met him as a boy, four years ago; he was Orchard Weaver. Before he could be stopped, he tossed a book, its pages flapped by the air as it fell, into the grave.

It was a newly printed volume titled "The Papers of the Ky Rebellion." As Forest—buried to his waist—thumbed through it, his benefactor shouted, "It's from Ayatsport Press, not the underground!" Being dragged away, the young man continued, "They're publishing it to initiate a test case, to seek absolute freedom of information!"

In the book were Infidel's most radical essays and a transcript of the interview Forest had given to River from his prison cell.

The last sapling was planted with the setting of the last sun, Monz, and the Garden entered the brief blackness of a spring night.

An observer in one of the Palace towers claimed that it was at that precise moment that candles were lighted in the Garden. No one has learned who brought them, who distributed them, or what they were intended to mean.

A pilot in one of the surveillance crocuses said that though their number decreased during the night, there were still many pinpoints of light, moving slowly in random patterns, when the first glow of Nya appeared in the east.

The navigator of a rocket taking off at about that time—a rocket carrying a construction crew and materials for rebuilding the staging depot at Syrdo—said he saw candles not only in the Garden but scattered here and there throughout the capital city.

The pilot of the same ship said that once they were too high to have seen candlelight, he fancied he saw a mystical illumination playing over the waves, the coastline, and extending across the dark land to the west. It was probably, he admitted, just an unusual condition of the dawn.

Another great science fiction novel by David Houston

LOOKING DOWN

A deadly disease has killed off all aboard an alien spacecraft except a handful of survivors sealed within the inner command sphere. The design of the craft makes it impossible for the aliens to get out or for aid to reach them without spreading the contagion. Finding themselves in the vicinity of Earth, but totally unfamiliar with the planet, the aliens decide to land and seek help.

If this book is not available at your local bookstore, send $1.75 plus 50¢ for shipping and handling to Leisure Books, P.O. Box 270, Norwalk, Conn. 06852.

ASSAULT ON BORDEAUX   LB570DK $1.50
B. J. Hurwood   War

Allied shipping in the North Atlantic was plagued by German submarines, based in the captured city of Bordeaux. They couldn't be attacked by air or sea. Or so the invaders thought! Four men set out to prove them wrong.

THE FREE AND THE BRAVE   LB591RK $2.25
John Cornwell   War

Not since CATCH-22 has there been a book that captures the war so well. Doomed to boring inactivity on the obsolete destroyer *Goddard*, George Kelly thought World War II would pass him by. Before long, he learned there was plenty of action—and danger—in the Caribbean!

DAWN COMMAND   LB600KK $1.75
Roland K. Jordon   War

The Pacific Fleet had been all but destroyed at Pearl Harbor, and there was nothing to threaten Japan's control of the seas. Nothing except the men whose bombers had survived the savage assault.

THE BATTERED BASTARDS   LB631 $1.75
Gordon French   War

In the middle of the heaviest action of the Battle of the Bulge, Sergeant Alan Bishop and his platoon of Screaming Eagles took what relief they could after six months in the front lines. Each one of them had his dreams—but they'd all settle for survival!
Setting: Bastogne, Belgium 1944

SGT. HAWK   LB640 $1.75
Patrick Clay   War

It was just another island in the Pacific to James Hawk and his Marines, another landing and another chance to kill Japanese—or be killed by them. But the Dutchman's plantation should have been a safe post for them, and, one by one, the Marines were being picked off!
Setting: the Pacific, 1943

HOLD SAIPAN!   LB614 $2.25
William Herber   War

Lieutenant Mike Andreas, U.S.M.C., had two jobs in front of him. The first one was tough—he had to convince his platoon of veterans that a green officer could lead them. The second job was impossible—he had to lead his men to the top of Mount Tapotchau on Japanese-held Saipan, and capture and hold the mountain!
Setting: Hawaii and Saipan, World War II

ACE OF SPIES   LB650 $1.75
Robin Bruce Lockhart   Adventure

Most espionage is done by anonymous men and women who work in back rooms of obscure ministries. The superspy who tracks down and stops the enemy singlehandedly is mostly a myth—except for Sidney Reilly, the British spy who changed the course of history!
Setting: Europe, World War I

THE HYDRA CONSPIRACY   LB655 $1.75
Philip Kirk   Adventure

Introducing Butler, the renegade ex-CIA agent who joins the fight to keep the U.S. out of the hands of the CIA and the military. In his first adventure, Butler confronts the super-secret and incredibly powerful organization known as Hydra!

SEND TO: LEISURE BOOKS
P.O. Box 270
Norwalk, Connecticut 06852

Please send me the following titles:

Quantity	Book Number	Price
_____	_____	_____
_____	_____	_____
_____	_____	_____
_____	_____	_____
_____	_____	_____

In the event we are out of stock on any of your selections, please list alternate titles below.

_____	_____	_____
_____	_____	_____
_____	_____	_____
_____	_____	_____

Postage/Handling _____

I enclose..... _____

FOR U.S. ORDERS, add 50¢ for the first book and 10¢ for each additional book to cover cost of postage and handling. Buy five or more copies and we will pay for shipping. Sorry, no C.O.D.'s.

FOR ORDERS SENT OUTSIDE THE U.S.A.
Add $1.00 for the first book and 25¢ for each additional book.
PAY BY foreign draft or money order drawn on a U.S. bank, payable in U.S. ($) dollars.
☐ Please send me a free catalog.

NAME _____
(Please print)

ADDRESS _____

CITY _____ STATE_____ ZIP _____
Allow Four Weeks for Delivery